FRACTURED SILENCE

A TALON PACK NOVEL

CARRIE ANN RYAN

Fractured Silence
A Talon Pack Novel

By
Carrie Ann Ryan

Fractured Silence
A Talon Pack Novel
By: Carrie Ann Ryan
© 2017 Carrie Ann Ryan
ISBN: 978-1-943123-53-7

This ebook is licensed for your personal enjoyment only. This ebook may not be re-sold or given away to other people. If you would like to share this book with another person, please purchase an additional copy for each person or use proper retail channels to lend a copy. If you're reading this book and did not purchase it, or it was not purchased for your use only, then please return it and purchase your own copy. Thank you for respecting the hard work of this author.
All characters in this book are fiction and figments of the author's imagination.

For more information, please join Carrie Ann Ryan's MAILING LIST.
To interact with Carrie Ann Ryan, you can join her FAN CLUB.

PRAISE FOR CARRIE ANN RYAN....

"Carrie Ann Ryan knows how to pull your heartstrings and make your pulse pound! Her wonderful Redwood Pack series will draw you in and keep you reading long into the night. I can't wait to see what comes next with the new generation, the Talons. Keep them coming, Carrie Ann!" –Lara Adrian, New York Times bestselling author of CRAVE THE NIGHT

"Carrie Ann Ryan never fails to draw readers in with passion, raw sensuality, and characters that pop off the page. Any book by Carrie Ann is an absolute treat." – New York Times Bestselling Author J. Kenner

"With snarky humor, sizzling love scenes, and brilliant, imaginative worldbuilding, The Dante's Circle series reads as if Carrie Ann Ryan peeked at my personal wish list!" – NYT Bestselling Author, Larissa Ione

"Carrie Ann Ryan writes sexy shifters in a world full of passionate happily-ever-afters." – *New York Times* Bestselling Author Vivian Arend

"Carrie Ann's books are sexy with characters you can't help but love from page one. They are heat and heart blended to perfection." *New York Times* Bestselling Author Jayne Rylon

"Carrie Ann Ryan's books are wickedly funny and deliciously hot, with plenty of twists to keep you guessing. They'll keep you up all night!" USA Today Bestselling Author Cari Quinn

"Once again, Carrie Ann Ryan knocks the Dante's Circle series out of the park. The queen of hot, sexy, enthralling paranormal romance, Carrie Ann is an author not to miss!" *New York Times* bestselling Author Marie Harte

DEDICATION

To my Miley. You sat with me for 53 books and cuddled me when I couldn't write anymore. I'm so sorry we lost you so young. You were my first kitten and a love of my life. You showed me true beauty and the art of caring. I miss you baby girl. For always.

ACKNOWLEDGMENTS

When I wrote the end to this book, it was the end of an era. Oh, this is totally not the end of the Talon Pack series, but the end of an arc I've been thinking about for four years. For those of you worried, there are still at least four more novels in the series with a whole new arc coming that has blown my mind and I cannot wait for you to read it.

But first, I need to thank a few people who helped me write the book. Thank you Team Carrie Ann—Chelle, Charity, Tara, and Dr. Hubby for helping me with every aspect of the production of this book. It truly takes a team and I love you guys.

Thank you to my BFF Kennedy Layne for kicking my butt when I didn't want to write and when I just wanted cake. Thank you to the Sprint Loop—Meredith Wild,

Stacey Kennedy, Kennedy Layne, Shayla Black, and those who popped in to help me keep my brain on my book.

And as always, thank you dear readers for going with me on this journey. I am truly blessed to have y'all in my life and I can't wait to see what books I get to write next!

Happy reading!

~Carrie Ann

FRACTURED SILENCE

The Talon Pack continues with a dark secret that could shatter the future of the Packs, or save them all.

Parker Jamenson is the son of three Packs, the sole mediator between every Pack in the United States and Europe, and...he's dying. He knows he doesn't have much left in him and is in desperate need of a mate. But with the new and unyielding changes thanks to the Moon Goddess, he might not have as much time as he thinks.

Brandon Brentwood is the Omega of the Talon Pack and the youngest of his family. He's not only one of the famed triplets; he's also the most secretive. There's a good reason for that, however, and when a shocking revelation meshes the past and present in a very unexpected way, he'll look to not only Parker but also a disgraced human to save them all.

Avery Montag knows she's the daughter of a traitor and doesn't have much to give the wolves in the way of atonement. But she'll do everything she can to pay for her father's sins and find a way to end the war between the humans and the wolves.

When the three turn to each other in a time of unrest and for vastly different reasons, temptation burns and seduction beckons. Only, the past, present, and future are never as solid as they seem, and the path the trio thought to travel may just vanish before they're ready.

CHAPTER 1

Before

PARKER JAMENSON WOKE with a start as someone knocked on the door to the small cabin he'd been staying in for the duration of his visit to this particular European Pack. Using his wolf's senses, he inhaled deeply, noting that the person on the other side of the door was one of the younger wolves that had shown him around when he'd first gotten there. He hadn't met most of the Pack, as the people of the den hadn't been too keen on his presence. He'd only just fallen asleep in the armchair fully clothed, exhausted from the trip.

He'd already spoken to the Alpha about coming

together with the Redwoods in times of war, but the damn man hadn't been too eager to reveal his existence to the world. All Alphas were required to meet with Parker as the Voice of the Wolves because he was goddess-touched, but that didn't mean they had to listen. Hell, most of them would rather bury their heads in the sand and ignore what was going on around them. And while his own Pack might be older than most in the United States, the European Packs were ancient and set in their ways. No one wanted to deal with the fact that the humans were aware of the shifters' existence, but Parker knew that soon, no one would have a choice.

He opened the door after a moment and nodded at the young woman on the other side. "Tatiana."

She smiled coyly at him before licking her lips. He could scent her wolf brushing up against her skin, wanting touch, but Parker wasn't interested. He just wanted to get this meeting with the elders over with and head back home. Her long, honey-colored hair had been in a braid when he'd first met her, but now it looked as if she'd brushed it out over her shoulders and back so it cascaded over her curves. She'd also put on a long, white, flowing dress instead of the tan one she'd worn when he'd shown up.

And though she looked to be his same age and her

power felt even younger, she dressed as if she were some maiden from a bygone era on the hunt for a knight.

Parker would not be that knight—no matter how much those eyes of hers flashed yearning.

"Parker," she breathed. "I'm to take you to the elder circle for your last meeting before you go." A pause. "It's a shame we didn't have more time to get to know one another while you were here. I understand you leave in the morning, but perhaps the meeting won't take long, and I can show you more of the grounds. I'm sure your wolf could use some exercise." She smiled. "And though it's not a full moon, there's just enough moonlight for the run to be…thrilling."

He held back a chuckle that wanted to spill out since that would have been rude. She wasn't hiding anything she wanted, and while he might have appreciated that on another day, he just wanted to go home. Besides, his wolf wasn't interested in the woman in front of him, and while that might not matter for a quick night of heat, he didn't have it in him to ignore his wolf tonight. *Maybe I'm getting older, and in need of a mate*, he thought. Or maybe he was just tired and missed his family. Either way, Tatiana wasn't for him.

"I'm afraid I will have to get ready to head out after the elder circle." He held back a frown at the crestfallen look on her face. They hadn't said more than a few words before this, and though he was a new wolf to her, he wasn't the only healthy adult male wolf around.

"I understand," she said softly. "Follow me, then." She turned without another word, but he didn't miss the extra sway to her hips—an invitation if he were to change his mind.

Keeping his thoughts to himself so he wouldn't inadvertently hurt her again if he were to change his mind—which he wouldn't—he followed her through the winding, dirt paths of the den toward the oldest part at the edge of the center. It made sense that this was where the elders chose to live—just slightly outside the most used part of the den for privacy but not near the edge in case of an attack. As elders, they were to not only be respected but also protected.

Tatiana left Parker with a nod, and he bent to walk under a low-lying branch so he could make it to the elder's circle. Encircling the firepit were seven older wolves of various sizes—three women and four men. At his entry, they all looked up as a unit and stared at him.

If he hadn't seen his own elders do this before, he would have been creeped out. Elder wolves were those who had either lost their mates long ago or had never been mated, so they didn't have a connection to the new world or the Pack except through their bonds to the Alpha and those in the hierarchy. After living for centuries, some wolves could no longer deal with the drastic changes of society and chose to cloister themselves. Many of the wolves held immense power on their own because of their age and used that strength to protect the Pack in any way they could.

Parker looked back at the elders respectfully. Though each of the wolves had at least two centuries on him, none of them looked a day over thirty-five. Wolf genetics never ceased to amaze him and he'd been born a wolf.

"Parker Jamenson, of the Redwoods," the woman closest to him said after a moment. "Welcome. I am Aurora. We're pleased you were able to take the time to meet with us before you head out on your journey home."

Parker bowed his head in deference. "I will always meet with my elders, Aurora. To ignore those who have lived the past is to ignore what the future may bring."

She smiled softly at his words and gestured for him to sit down before introducing him to the others. He kept their names in the back of his mind, but he knew that it was Aurora who led here, and she would be the one to speak.

"We've asked you to join us because we believe we have something that once belonged to your people. Your line."

Parker's eyes widened. "The Redwoods?" How did something of theirs find its way here?

"Not that line." Aurora's eyes went gold, her wolf rising to the surface. "The line of the first hunter. You are the son of the son of the son of the line of the first hunter, are you not?"

Parker froze. Not many people knew that his family came from that line. In fact, he'd only recently learned that his ancestor was the first human to be made into a wolf by the moon goddess as a punishment for what the man had done to defenseless prey. She'd forced the man to become the thing he killed for sport, compelled him to share a soul with that of a wolf. From there, new wolves were made, and shifters were born.

His uncle, Logan, had dealt with horrible side effects from that past, but other than his strength, Parker hadn't really thought about what that meant. Logan had been far too aggressive even at a young age, and it had taken him years to learn how to fully control his wolf. He, like Parker, had also had to learn how to use their strength wisely when they'd been mere pups and still had to deal with some bursts of overextension some days. The family bloodline was diluted over time, and Parker had had more recent issues with it thanks to his birth father. His mother might be of the line of their honorable ancestors and campfire stories, but his birth father had been one of nightmares. He'd never truly met the man as he'd been young when Corbin died, but he knew the stories. Knew that the former Central Alpha had killed countless in his quest for power.

He pushed that thought out of his head, as he knew just letting it in would enrage him.

"I'm of that line, yes," he answered after a moment. No need to lie as he had a feeling these wolves knew far more than this. "What did you find?" he asked.

Aurora nodded at one of the male wolves after Parker had spoken. The male stood up with shaky hands, a large box wrapped in cloth clasped between them.

Aurora took it gently from him. "This box is made of the woods of our people—Redwood, Aspen, Oak, and so forth. It is said those first Packs, along with the first ever, came together to make it."

Parker frowned. "What's in the box?"

"Open it and see."

Though his wolf had stood at attention as soon as they'd mentioned the box, it wasn't until Aurora unwrapped it—keeping her hands on the cloth rather than the wood—that his wolf howled.

He frowned. "I'm not going to open something I haven't looked into with wolves I don't know. I'm sorry if that's disrespectful, but that just doesn't seem like a good idea to me."

Aurora's eyes flashed, but he had a feeling it was more

out of respect than anger. "It's good you're cautious. That will help."

"Help what?"

"There is a prophecy," she said after a moment.

He blinked. "A prophecy?" Why did he feel like he'd suddenly jumped into an old Indiana Jones movie?

Aurora's eyes unfocused as she spoke in a deeper voice.

"*A wolf of three Packs can break their will or unite them all.*

"*Once united, the Packs will reveal...*

"*If broken, the Packs will fall...*"

Parker's wolf rushed to the surface at her words, and he tried to blink, attempted to reach out and catch the woman as she fell forward after she'd finished speaking. Only he felt as if he were moving slower than usual, his mind not quite where it should be. His hand brushed the top of the box, and it slid to the ground, opening on impact.

He looked down, his head going fuzzy, his mouth dry.

An ancient dagger, or perhaps the tip of a spear, rolled out of the box amidst a dust cloud that slapped at his face.

"The weapon of the first hunter," Aurora croaked before passing out completely. The others surrounded them, yet he could do nothing but try to keep himself upright.

Parker tried to speak but couldn't force his mouth to work. Instead, his body broke out in a cold sweat, and he fell face-first to the ground.

The last thing he thought about before passing out was his family.

They weren't here to help him.

No one was here to help him.

He was all alone.

And it was his fault.

Again.

Now

THE WORLD HADN'T ENDED, BUT IT DAMN WELL FELT as if it were on the brink of something cataclysmic. Parker swirled the aged scotch in his glass, wondering why he'd been all the way over in Europe and not home in his den, helping his Pack through the end of the world.

Through their Unveiling.

He'd watched the screen with the rest of the world as their Pack's ally, the Talon Pack, fought for their lives and were forced out into the open. Shifters were real and had been living amongst the humans for far longer than anyone could have imagined.

And when the witches were forced out into the open thanks to greed and death, Parker had been on his own once again, far away from home. Deep inside, he knew that even if he had been home, nothing would have changed. He was just one wolf against a world that had come to the point in their existence when they could no longer accept the secrets that had alluded them for centuries. Yet he hadn't been by his family members' sides through their struggles. He'd missed countless matings, births, and losses, but he knew he couldn't change a damn thing. He was on an important mission—far greater than one man, one Pack. Though that didn't make things any easier.

He sighed, the melancholy running through his veins sickening.

He might not have been home when the war started, but he knew now that he *was* home, he could do something. He'd spent years visiting the Packs to reaffirm their ties to each other so he could return to the Redwoods. And while technology had advanced tremendously, and Parker should have been able to do all of it via satellite, he knew that none of the wolves of old would allow that. Meetings of such importance and tradition had to be done face-to-face so their wolves could assert their relative strength of dominance.

Parker was born of three Packs, the son of a traitor on

one side and a fighter on the other. His wolf was far more dominant than many of the Alphas he'd met, and yet, he knew he would never be Alpha. He didn't want to. He was born to be a mediator thanks to the blood in his veins, and that was what he did now as the Voice of the Wolves.

With a sigh, he rolled his head over his shoulders and thought of what it felt like to be home. After leaving for each meeting with the elders and Alphas of other Packs, he knew he'd return to his families different than how he'd left them.

From what his family had told him, the Redwoods and the Talons were slowly becoming one Pack through their treaties and matings. *Perhaps that's best,* Parker thought. With the war reaching a tipping point with the humans, perhaps having two Alphas with the strength of two Packs behind them would give the wolves a chance. It wasn't about sheer strength anymore, and most of the wolves he'd met with had understood that. They needed diplomacy, as well as backdoor deals with higher officials—something they'd slowly been working into place over time. Humans didn't know that the wolves had infiltrated their inner workings, wearing sheep's clothing of politicians and lobbyists in Washington. Between using real wolves who blended in so well that unless you scented them you couldn't tell they had a predator prowling beneath their skin, and human mates of wolves with connections, their kind had people in the right places within the government to ensure that they wouldn't be outright slaughtered.

They'd seen the writing on the wall years ago and had done what they could to ensure that their people wouldn't die at the hands of those who didn't understand them. Yet, Parker wasn't sure it would be enough.

He wasn't sure *he* would be enough.

And that was enough of that. He didn't have time to wallow, not anymore. He stood up and stretched before downing the rest of his scotch and deciding he needed a walk outside to clear his mind. It wasn't as if the alcohol would do much for him thanks to his wolf metabolism. He just liked the taste. He'd spent a few days at his parents' home, but he knew it was time to leave. It wasn't safe for them if he stayed, and he'd tempted fate long enough.

It wasn't safe for anyone.

Parker coughed, annoyed that he'd let that weakness slip, but he couldn't help it. His body was failing him, and there would only be so much time before he'd have to tell his family the truth about what had happened when he was away. Thankfully, he stood on a path near his parents' home in the Redwood den and not somewhere more populous, but wolves had too keen ears most days.

His parents' the keenest.

"Are you done moping?" his younger brother, Blake,

asked as he strolled toward him. "You've been here a few days now, and yet I've only seen you growl and brood like some teenage heartthrob trying to get a girl."

"I don't brood," he said calmly, holding back a smile at Blake's words. Parker had been sixteen when his sister Isabelle was born, and eighteen when Blake came along. Though they were technically half-siblings, it hadn't much mattered in how they treated each other. He'd been calling North his father since the man mated his mother, and no blood ties could change that.

"You brood. Often." Blake stuck his hands in his pockets and rocked back on his heels. "You're really going to live with the Talons? You just got here, Park, and now you're jet-setting off again."

Parker resisted the urge to rub a hand over his heart at the hurt in Blake's tone. "It's for the best, Blake."

Blake's brows furrowed. "You keep saying that, but you never tell us why. You just say you should be another liaison since you're part of the council with the Talons, but hell, you can do that kind of thing in our den, can't you?"

Parker had been part of the original council formed over fifteen years ago that had brokered the first settlings of true partnership between the Redwoods and Talons. Though other members had come and gone, he'd always been a part of it—even if he hadn't been in the den for long periods of time.

"I have to go, Blake." His words were low, not a growl but close. He couldn't tell them why he couldn't stay, but they had to know it was for a good reason. He wouldn't leave them otherwise.

Isabelle bounced over, her long, brown hair flowing behind her. While Parker might look somewhat like the two younger wolves, Isabelle and Blake looked like twins—even if they were two years apart. He still couldn't believe his baby brother and sister were adults in their early twenties now, with positions in the Pack and everything.

Time flew when you had the potential to live centuries.

"Mom and Dad said you'd packed the car already," Isabelle said as she went to his side. Parker immediately backed away, hating himself for the hurt he'd put on her face. "Crap. Sorry, I forgot." She gave him a searching look and then leaned into Blake as he put his arm around her shoulders.

"That's why I need to go," Parker said suddenly, aware he would say too much if he weren't careful. He hadn't hugged his family or gone wolf with them in the two days he'd been back. While he might be standing right then and able to breathe, whatever had been in or on that box back at the European den had shaken him. And if it was because of the blood in his veins, there was no way he'd spread it to the other members of his family.

"I know you're not going far, but you'll call, right?" Isabelle asked, her eyes filling. She was a submissive wolf, one that needed to be protected above all others, though he knew she had a spine of steel, as well. Blake, on the other hand, was a dominant like Parker.

Hence the fire in the younger man's eyes.

"Every day," Parker promised. "Every damn day."

Isabelle raised her chin. "Good. Because I'll kick your butt if you don't." A pause. "Or I'll get Blake to do it and distract you so it actually works."

"Hey," Blake put in, clearly offended. "I don't need a distraction to take Parker down."

Parker held back a smile as the two play-fought, knowing he needed to find a cure for whatever ailed him, and soon. There was no way he'd be able to live with himself if he lost his siblings because of what had happened to him.

Knowing he couldn't hug them goodbye, he said his farewells softly, having already done so with his parents earlier. Neither of them had probed too much into the reasons Parker needed to be away, which had surprised him. At least until later when North had cornered him.

"We know enough about secrets, Park," North had

said softly. "Goddess knows our family has had enough of them. Just know that we're here for you. Always."

It had taken everything inside him for Parker to leave after that.

But he had no choice.

Not then, and surely not now.

After leaving the others staring at his retreat, Parker drove the distance to the Talon den. Over time, the distance had shortened as the dens grew and the neutral area between them became smaller. There were other ways to get into the dens that were hidden from humans, but the stretch of road he was on now was constantly patrolled and relatively safe. Still, his wolf was on alert just in case.

Thankfully, the trip was uneventful and left Parker to his thoughts. Though, really, he probably shouldn't be left alone with those as often as he was. As he was waved through the sentries and wards that kept the den safe, he noticed how much had been cleaned up since the battle that had cost everyone so much. He'd literally stepped off the plane and into the chaos of his best friend's and cousin's mating, kidnapping, and the battle that had included a freaking *tank*.

He'd fought alongside the Talon wolves, and a certain wolf in particular, who apparently couldn't stand the sight of him. That would make living in the den near him interesting.

Gideon, the Talon Alpha, waited for him as Parker turned off his vehicle. He slid out of the car and closed the door behind him. While Parker knew his wolf was dominant, he had nothing on Gideon. The wolf bled power and strength, and yet he'd mated Parker's *very* submissive cousin.

It never failed to surprise Parker how the moon goddess and fate liked to test the waters of the impossible.

"Good to see you, Parker," the Alpha said, holding out his hand.

Parker shook it, his wolf bowing his head. There was a clear line of dominance here, and he wasn't about to mess with anything as he was just a guest.

"Thanks for letting me stay." *And for not asking questions.*

Gideon shrugged. "Over the past couple of years, a few of my wolves have ended up either in matings or close enough friendships that they now live in the Redwood den and vice versa. It's not a hardship to have a strong wolf living with us." Gideon met Parker's eyes, and Parker did his best not to flinch. Hell, this guy was an *Alpha*, much like Parker's uncle, Kade. "And you know how to behave and not get into dominance fights in the middle of another den with your position as Voice of the Wolves. So we're not going to have any trouble."

If that wasn't a warning, Parker didn't know what was.

"Either way, thank you."

Gideon nodded. "With so many of our people back in the den since the Unveiling, we're short on extra single bunks. I'm putting you with another wolf who could use a roommate."

There wasn't a question anywhere in that statement, so Parker didn't nod in agreement, but he couldn't help but ask the question, "And they're fine with me staying with them?"

Gideon snorted, a smile playing on his face that didn't make him look any less deadly. Seriously, how did Brie deal with the man on a daily basis? And with her pregnant, Parker assumed he just got worse as the months progressed.

"He will be."

Hairs on the back of his neck stood up. "Who exactly am I staying with?"

"Brandon, my younger brother. The Omega of our Pack."

Parker froze. Brandon. The wolf he'd saved on the battlefield…and the one wolf he knew couldn't stand the sight of him.

Yes, this was definitely going to be interesting.

CHAPTER 2

"I CAN'T BELIEVE he went behind my back and did this," Brandon Brentwood growled.

His cousin Mitchell snorted. "He's Alpha and in a growly mood since Brie is gonna pop soon. Of course, he did this."

Brandon stuffed another set of clothes he needed to wash in the hamper and held back a growl of his own. "Why couldn't he stay with you? You have the extra space."

Something flickered over Mitchell's gaze, and Brandon held back a shocked moan. As the Omega, Brandon could sense the emotions of those in his Pack without even thinking about it. It had taken him a few years after coming into his powers to learn to block the daily emotions of others so he could actually breathe. It was only during times of truly strong emotions that Brandon sometimes felt overwhelmed. Mitchell was always so locked-up and cold that Brandon usually had difficulty figuring out if his cousin, his Beta, felt anything at all.

Except, in that moment, Brandon had gotten a mere glimpse of what lay beneath the surface of the man.

And he wasn't sure he could handle finding out more.

Mitchell raised his chin, seemingly aware that he'd let something slip before moving on. "Gideon seems to think you shouldn't be alone anymore. And from the way your jeans are falling off your hips, and the look of the bags under your eyes, I'm inclined to agree with him."

Brandon flipped him off. "I'm fine."

"That's what someone who is clearly *not* fine would say," Mitchell drawled. "There is something going on with you, and you're not talking about it with us. Maybe we're too close to you, or maybe you just need someone else near you that's not connected to you through Pack bonds." Mitchell met Brandon's gaze, his eyes rimmed with gold, letting everyone know that his wolf was close to the surface. "We all know what happens to Omegas who go too long without a mate. We didn't have an Omega in the Pack before Gideon became Alpha and our Pack started to heal again, but the Redwoods told us what happened to Maddox before he found Ellie. Even though Maddox isn't the true Omega anymore since the next generation took their places, he's still someone you can talk to."

Brandon turned away and finished cleaning up the guest room where Parker would be sleeping from now on. "Just drop it, okay? I'm not going to die because I don't have a mate. That's not how these things work."

"No, you'll just become insane because you don't have the ability to handle all the crushing emotions. Maybe it should have taken longer to hit you, but hell, we're in the middle of a damn war the likes of which we never could have imagined. So, yeah, emotions are running high, and it's taking you apart, bit by bit."

Brandon turned on his heel, facing his cousin. "Like it's not affecting you? Come on. You're barely getting any sleep these days, making sure Gideon doesn't carry too much of a burden. His mate is about to give birth, and our Heir, Ryder, is newly mated and dealing with his own problems. We're all handling far too much, and yet I'm the only one getting a babysitter."

"I'm not planning to spy on you for your brother, if that helps at all."

Brandon twisted at the sound of Parker's voice, his claws poking out from his fingertips and his fangs ready to descend from his gums. He inhaled the clean scent of Parker that always seemed to get under his skin and forced himself to relax. He'd been so focused on Mitchell and getting the mess of his house ready, that he hadn't noticed Parker come in. Inattentiveness like that could get a wolf killed, and he knew he'd have to get his head on straight. No wonder Gideon wanted Parker there. It seemed that Brandon couldn't even act like a normal wolf and know who was on his territory at any given moment.

"Good to know," Brandon bit out, still annoyed with himself. His wolf pressed at him before pulling back, not interested in what was going on any longer.

Parker pointed back the way he'd come. "I knocked, but nobody answered, and I heard you guys back here."

His hand gripped the hamper tighter as he studied the man in front of him; aware that Mitchell was still in the room, looking at them both. Parker was not only taller than Brandon, but wider, too—packed full of muscle. Though Brandon could have sworn Parker had been even larger than he was now. Was the other man losing weight? Parker had once again neglected to cut his shaggy, brown hair, but the style suited his features and only emphasized his hazel eyes. The man was seriously attractive, and if his wolf had given him any indication that it was intrigued, Brandon figured Parker would be interesting in bed.

But his wolf remained silent, and Brandon didn't have time to sleep with wolves who weren't potential mates. It didn't matter that he found the man far too sexy for his own good. He needed to find a mate and create a bond soon, or Mitchell's premonition would come true, and Brandon would find himself insane under the weight of his duty and his responsibility as Omega.

"I'll leave you both to it, then," Mitchell said after a moment before turning to Parker. "And remember, wolf, you're a guest here on our land. Don't fuck with my cousin, and I won't have to fuck with you."

Parker tilted his head as he studied Mitchell, a move so wolf-like that Brandon knew Parker's beast was close to the surface. "Is that how you treat all of your guests, Beta?"

"Only the ones that I might like. The others don't get a chance." And with that, Mitchell strolled away, leaving Brandon alone in the room with Parker.

"Your cousin seems like a real nice guy," Parker said dryly after a moment.

"There's a reason he's not usually on the welcoming committee." Brandon loosened his grip on the hamper and tried to keep the awkward feeling in the room from getting to him. He hadn't had a roommate since he'd moved out at the age of eighteen, and he wasn't sure he knew what to do with one now. Up until he'd left, he'd shared a small room that held a tiny twin bed and twin bunk beds with his fellow triplets, Walker and Kameron. While some families might have let their adult kids live with them until they were ready to move out, Brandon's family wasn't anywhere near *normal*.

He and Parker stared at each other for a few moments before Parker cleared his throat. "I know you don't want me here, and when Gideon agreed that I could stay here for a bit, I didn't know he meant *here*. I thought there would be room in the soldier's barracks or he'd pitch me a tent in the woods or something."

Brandon let out a breath. It wasn't Parker's fault that he'd been forced to stay with Brandon thanks to the meddling Alpha, and he shouldn't take it out on the man. Oh, there might be some lingering resentment about what had happened on the battlefield, but that didn't have to do with what was going on in the room now. Or at least, it shouldn't. It wasn't his fault the other man had tried to save him. It was his fault he hadn't been fast enough to begin with.

"You're fine to stay here. A lot of the single males are bunking in the barracks, and the single females are all doubled or tripled up. We're in the process of making new homes—or at least we *were* until General Montag kept attacking our den—but until that happens, we're all a little cramped." Brandon set down the hamper and ran a hand over his face, aware he was starting to sweat. There was something coming that he couldn't quite get a handle on yet and his wolf was on edge. If he didn't sit down soon—away from Parker's prying eyes—he might reveal too much.

"You should still have your space, Brandon. You're the Omega."

"Yeah, and I usually need the space to clear out the emotions that get clogged up after a long day in the den. But we're not Packmates, so I can't actually feel your emotions. It'll be like you're not even here."

Parker raised a brow, and Brandon had a feeling they both knew that what he'd just said was a lie. From the curious glances they'd given each other since they'd first met, he knew they were both interested, but as he said before…he wasn't going down that path—not with someone who couldn't be his mate.

He just didn't have the time.

"Glad I won't be in the way, then. Is this where you want me to stay?"

He didn't want Parker anywhere near him, but Brandon kept that to himself. "Yeah, sorry about the mess. I've been throwing things in here after I work out since the guest shower has better pressure. I'm not the tidiest of wolves."

Parker let out a soft laugh. "I'm not as *tidy*—as you put it—as some of my family either, but I'll do my best to keep whatever mess I make contained to this room." He paused. "Again, I'm sorry for putting myself in your way. I just…I just need to stay away from my family."

Brandon's brows rose. That was the exact opposite thing he would have expected Parker to say. The Jamensons were all close. Like annoyingly close and caring. Of course, they hadn't gone through what the Brentwoods did with their previous Alpha—Brandon's father. Each Pack had their own wars, but they'd come out stronger because of it. Brandon was only just now seeing their true strengths as his family rose from the ashes of their past betrayals.

"You going to explain that?" Brandon gritted out.

"You going to explain why you look like death warmed over?" Parker shot back.

Brandon raised his chin, annoyed to no end with this wolf for just *existing*. "Thanks for that. Does wonders for the self-esteem. Here's your fucking room. You get the general idea. I have things to do other than welcome the crowned Redwood prince into my home. I'm sure you can find your way around."

With that, he stormed around Parker, being sure to run into the man's arm with his shoulder. He'd spent far too long just then staring at the man and finding him attractive, but apparently, Brandon wasn't good enough for Parker.

He cursed under his breath and made his way to his room, stripping off his shirt as he went since he still needed to shower. He shouldn't care if Parker found him attractive or not. Hell, it shouldn't matter at all. Yet, for some reason, he was beyond annoyed and even a little hurt that he didn't sense an attraction.

Maybe his Omega bonds were truly on the verge of making him insane if this was how he reacted to a mere taunt.

"Shit, Brandon, I'm sorry. I didn't mean to lash out like that."

Brandon turned as Parker stopped in the doorway, his gaze on Brandon's chest rather than his face. At least that reaction seemed to assuage the hurt of whatever had happened back in the other room, but it didn't do much in terms of Brandon's confusion. What was going on with him?

"It's fine," Brandon bit out, nausea washing over him. It wasn't a reaction to Parker, but something far darker. His legs shook, and sweat poured down his back, his hands going clammy. "Shit." His knees finally gave out, and he fell forward, only to land hard against Parker's broad chest.

"What's wrong? Talk to me."

Brandon gripped Parker's biceps, resting his forehead on the other man's collarbone as he fought to catch his breath. "The wards," Brandon gritted out, panting. "They're having another flare."

"I've got you," Parker said softly, holding Brandon to him, steady, unyielding. "What can I do?"

Brandon hated relying on anyone and would rather do this on his own—whatever *this* was—instead of letting a wolf that continually got under his skin help him. Yet he wasn't sure he had a choice at the moment, not when he was this weak.

With each roll of the wards, his body felt as if it were being torn apart. He didn't understand why his connection to the failing wards seemed to be stronger than the others', but he wasn't in a position to do anything about it. Until they could find a way to ensure that the witches could strengthen the wards and keep his people safe, his reaction to their failing would continue to happen.

And there was nothing he could do about it.

Yet he couldn't lie and say that having someone to lean on, even if only for this moment, hurt. It was the exact opposite, actually. Was this what it was like to have a mate? To have someone who would be there for you no matter what pained you?

Another crash of unending pain and bile rose in his throat.

No, this wasn't like a mating, not even close. This was just the one time he couldn't hide his reaction to the failings of the Pack's magic. His body shuddered as the ward flare ended and the dimming of his vision dissipated. It would seem hiding what he'd been going through for months wouldn't be easy with a roommate.

Parker looked down at him with an intense focus in his eyes.

Easy, hell it might not be possible at all.

It took a few more minutes, but finally, Brandon was able to stand on his own. Why Parker hadn't simply lain him down on the ground, Brandon didn't know, but his wolf had enjoyed the way Parker held him close. If he hadn't been confused about what was going on between them before, he sure was now.

"Better?" Parker asked, his voice low.

"Yeah." Brandon cleared his throat and pulled away, putting sufficient distance between them. "Thanks."

"I'd say no problem, but it seems to be a pretty big problem. Don't you think?"

Brandon let out a breath. "It's the wards, Parker. Just let it be."

"So the others don't know that every time your wards flare, threatening to fail just like all the other wards in the country are threatening to do, you end up passed out in excruciating pain?"

"Just let it be," he repeated, his voice pleading.

Parker searched Brandon's face before seeming to come to some kind of agreement within himself. "For now. But if it gets worse, you tell me. And if it happens again when I'm in the house with you, call for me. Or, hell, I'll probably hear you anyway so just let me help you get through it."

"And if I don't agree?" Brandon bit out. He didn't appreciate being backed into a corner.

"Then I go right to Gideon or one of your other brothers. Hell, I'll call Brynn since she's mated to my cousin and I see her more than I see the rest of you. I know you'll probably hate me for forcing this on you, but you can't do this alone."

Brandon let out a curse. He didn't see another way out of this, and his wolf *had* needed the help. He didn't have to like it, though. "Fine. I need to shower…like I was planning to do."

Parker searched his face but didn't object. "I'll start unpacking." He paused. "Thank you again. I…I needed to be close to my family, my Pack, my den, but not too close."

Brandon narrowed his eyes, impatience crawling up his spine. "You're going to have to tell me what you mean by that at some point." He held up his hands when Parker opened his mouth to most likely object. "Not now. But soon. Holding in whatever you've been hiding for too long will only hurt you in the long run."

Parker looked at him for a moment before shaking his head, a small smile playing on his face. "You're one to talk, Omega. Go shower. I'll unpack. Then we'll see where we're at."

Brandon watched the other man walk away, aware that everything had once again changed now that Parker was living under the same roof as him. Another wave of nausea hit him, and he turned, scrambling to the bathroom to empty the contents of his stomach. His body shook, and he dry-heaved until there was nothing left. He kept his eyes closed, sickened at how weak he felt because of the connection a goddess—whom he had never met—had put on him. If he were any other wolf, he'd be healthy and whole, able to fight and protect his family. Instead, he was weak, still healing from the gunshot wound he'd received in battle, and annoyed about a new and unbonded wolf in his territory.

When a cool washcloth pressed to the back of his neck, he wasn't surprised. He just leaned in to the touch, taking what comfort he could.

"Again?" Parker asked.

"No," Brandon croaked. "Same wave, just the aftermath."

"Shit," Parker mumbled. "This is killing you."

"We're all dying," he said dryly. "Just some faster than others."

Parker froze by his side before moving the washcloth to Brandon's hand. "You seem to have stopped shaking, so a shower might be in order. I'll meet you in the kitchen when you're done."

Unnerved, Brandon looked up and once again watched Parker walk out of the room. There was something seriously off about that wolf, yet Brandon couldn't put a finger on what.

Annoyed with himself for once again showing weakness to an unknown wolf in his territory, Brandon pushed himself up before stripping off his jeans and underwear. He walked naked to the shower and turned on the spray, sighing when he remembered the lack of water pressure in this bathroom. That was why he usually showered in the guest room. It looked like he'd have to find a way to fix it in here or he'd never be able to truly enjoy a shower in his own home.

He quickly went about his business, washing off the sweat and stink of being sick and dressed in a pair of sweats, keeping his chest bare. He worried for a minute if he should put a shirt on since he had a guest, but he pushed that thought out of his mind. He barely had a sense of who he was these days and didn't want to lose the only thing he had left—his space. So he decided to do what he normally did around the house and go shirtless. Parker would just have to deal with it. He quickly brushed his teeth and sighed, knowing he had to leave the bathroom soon and stop hiding.

Hungry, he went into the kitchen and made himself a protein shake. While something else might have been tastier, his body was in need of more nutrients than usual these days. Remembering the dark circles under Parker's eyes, he made a large batch, aware he might be crossing a boundary but not particularly caring. They weren't real roommates, weren't lovers or mates. Providing food for another wolf was an act that could be construed as something neither of them wanted, but he did it anyway.

He was just pouring the second helping into a glass when Parker walked in, his hand rubbing over the hard ridges of his abs through his thin shirt. Though Brandon had never touched Parker's stomach, he knew they'd be hard. Hell, he knew all of Parker would be hard.

He quickly adjusted himself in his sweats. And that was enough of that line of thinking.

"Thought you could use a shake," Brandon said after a moment.

Parker met his gaze and nodded. "Thanks."

They both sipped, their gazes never leaving one another, and Brandon knew that each of them held their own secrets. He just didn't know what to do about it.

Brandon's phone beeped, breaking their connection. He looked at the readout and frowned. "Gideon wants me at the sentry gate and says to bring you with me." He tossed back the last of his shake and looked around for a spare shirt before belatedly remembering that he'd cleaned up the place for Parker. "I need to put on some shoes and a shirt, and I'll be ready to go."

Parker frowned. "He's not my Alpha," the other wolf said.

"You're here at his pleasure," Brandon put in. "And Gideon orders everyone around."

Parker shook his head. "Sounds like pretty much every dominant wolf I know."

That made Brandon smile. "Pretty much." He ran back to his room and pulled on the first shirt he could find before sliding on socks and boots. It took him a little longer than it would have if he'd thrown on sneakers, and the boots probably looked ridiculous with his sweats, but he wanted to be prepared in case he had to leave the den for an emergency with whatever Gideon needed.

"Let's go," he said once he came back into the kitchen.

Parker nodded, and the two of them quickly made their way to the sentry gate as instructed. The Talon den wasn't as large land-wise as the Redwood den since the Pack wasn't as big, but usually, people drove from place to place if it was a long enough distance. Thankfully, Brandon's home was closer to the sentry gate than most of his siblings'.

When they arrived, Gideon was already there with Kameron—their Enforcer—and a few of the Lieutenants including Shane, their newest recruit.

"What's up?" Brandon asked, Parker on his tail.

"There's a woman outside who says she wants to speak to the Alpha," Gideon answered.

Brandon frowned. "Is she human?"

"Yep," Kameron put in. "And, well…we wanted to gauge your reaction when she tells you who she is."

Brandon's brows shot up. "I'm only connected emotionally to the Talons."

"Yeah, but you're a hell of a lot more empathic than the rest of us," Shane added.

"Okay."

"Bring Parker with you," Gideon ordered before looking at the other man. "You're not empathic, but you're a good judge of character and have met more wolves and those connected to wolves than any other person I know."

Parker frowned along with Brandon but gave a quick nod.

Confused, Brandon moved toward the gate to see who was there. Because the wards protected them from outsiders, whoever was on the other side wouldn't be able to see him until he slid through to the other side. From the way the others acted, he knew this wasn't a trap, but there was still something hinky about it. Back in the day, when the wards were working perfectly, humans wouldn't even be able to sense that they were there but would automatically be compelled to go the opposite direction. But as his body's weakened state attested, the wards were anything but healthy.

Brandon slid through the wards, Parker at his side, and exhaled roughly at the sight of a gorgeous woman with long, dark hair and bright, green eyes. She was all curves and strength, and if he didn't know better, he'd have thought her a wolf. She had what looked to be a camera bag at her hip and a backpack on her back. There were two sentries beside her, keeping guard.

When the two wolves moved forward, her eyes widened, but she didn't take a step back.

"You're not the Alpha," she said after a moment.

Interesting, Gideon hadn't been out to meet her, then. Since the Unveiling, any Alphas that had been revealed were easily recognizable thanks to the media. He must have only looked at her through the wards, keeping his distance until he knew what was going on. That was a true test for an Alpha—allowing others to stand beside you while you made sure the den was safe.

"No, I'm not," Brandon said smoothly. "But why don't you tell me who *you* are."

The woman's jaw clenched, but she gave him a tight nod. "I'm Avery Montag."

The last name made Brandon freeze, ice filling his veins. "Any relation to General Montag?" The man who had single-handedly massacred over a hundred wolves and started a war; a conflict that had taken Montag's life but was still ongoing. The man had not only studied wolves by torturing them before ending their lives, he'd also created a serum that was supposed to create shifters. Only it hadn't worked as intended and had nearly killed Shane in the process.

Montag was also the man who had been in charge of the latest attack on their den, bringing a freaking *tank* to try and destroy their wards. If they had truly fallen, their weakest and most vulnerable would have had one less layer of protection against those who would see them dead.

"He was my father."

"Shit," Parker whispered, so low that only a wolf would have been able to hear. Brandon had a feeling, however, that Avery knew what their reactions would be.

"I want to help," Avery rushed out "Please. I just want to help."

Brandon studied the woman, unsure what the hell all of this meant. She could be here for any number of reasons, yet his wolf wanted to trust her. Why, he didn't know. But what he *did* know was that things had just gotten truly interesting.

And *interesting* for a dying wolf could only mean one thing.

Disaster.

CHAPTER 3

AVERY MONTAG DID her best not to lower her gaze from the two hulking men in front of her, though she didn't meet their eyes either. She'd read about wolves and their dominance games. She was just a human, and there was no way she wanted to challenge them by just meeting their gazes. However, she also refused to lower her chin in a sign of true submission. That left her with her head held high but her eyes not directly on theirs. She just hoped that was good enough.

"How do we know you're not here to finish what your father started?" the larger man asked, his voice almost a growl.

She did her best to ignore the insane shivers that rolled over her at the sound of his words. There was clearly something wrong with her if she was thinking about how sexy they both sounded instead of running away from the big, bad predators.

"I'm not my father." She'd said that to herself countless times, whispering it in the dead of night when she had nothing left. She'd thought it for years, using it as a talisman to ward off the darkness before her mother had been killed. Then, when she'd lost it all, she'd said it daily—only never aloud to another soul.

Until now.

She wasn't her father. She wasn't a monster.

She was just a woman who needed to atone for the sins of her father.

Nothing unusual there.

The other man tilted his head, studying her as a wolf might. These two clearly weren't human, even though they looked it. They were too large, too in-tune with everything around them. How anyone could mistake them for anything but...*more*, she didn't know.

Of course, no one knew she was different either—even if she were a special kind of unique.

She was good at hiding what she was. She had to be. Only now that she'd put herself in the middle of a war she wasn't sure she fully comprehended, she had a feeling she wouldn't be hiding for much longer. As she'd said before, these two saw too much.

And they would soon be able to see *her* if they looked hard enough.

The smaller one—if you could count the six-foot, muscled man in front of her *small*—frowned.

"She's right, she's not her father," he said softly. "I think we should let her speak to Gideon once she tells us what exactly she means by *help*."

She tried not to show her cards by looking too relieved, but she couldn't help it. She let out a breath and adjusted the camera on her hip. "I have a few ideas, but really, I'm here to do whatever you need me to. I know that what's happening to your people is wrong, and I want you to know that not all humans want to see the end of the shifters." She was rambling at this point since she didn't have a clear plan. She only knew she needed to figure out something to show the human world that shifters were just people with their own set of rules—regulations that didn't necessarily go against the human ones. She wasn't sure that would be enough for the Alpha of a Pack of shifters, though.

What she was sure of...she'd been out of her mind when she'd seen the battle on-screen a few nights ago. She'd witnessed the pain and agony of so many because of one man: her father. And when she'd seen her dad die at the hands of those he'd tried to butcher, it hadn't been sadness for the man she'd felt—but relief.

What kind of daughter did that make her, if she weren't sad that her father was dead but sad for those he'd hurt along the way?

Not a daughter he could be proud of, that much was true—he'd said it over and over throughout her younger years. And yet she was just fine with that. Any daughter that cruel being could be proud of was not a person she wanted to be.

She narrowed her eyes at the two men, something from her memory coming back in an instant. "You were shot," she gaped at the shorter man. "I remember seeing it." She looked at the larger one, not taking care to avoid their gazes as she did. "And you were the one who tried to get him off the field."

The man who'd been shot growled low as the larger man sighed.

"That was us," the larger man said. "I'm Parker Jamenson. This is Brandon Brentwood. He doesn't like when you mention that I saved his life."

"I was doing just fine without you," Brandon bit out.

Okay, then. It looked like she'd stepped into something that wasn't her business. Again. But as a photojournalist, that was kind of her job.

Brandon growled again before looking past Parker at a dense section of woods. The same thick copse the two men had magically appeared through when they'd first shown up and the two guards flanking her had blended away. Those must be the wards everyone was talking about online—the ones that humans couldn't see, which kept the wolves safe. She didn't blame the Packs for using them one bit. With so many people confused or out to get them, they needed any type of protection they could get.

"There's something about her, but she's sincere as far as I can tell."

She wasn't sure whom Brandon was talking to until an even *larger* man stepped through the trees. Were all shifters this big, or were these just her welcoming committee? And what had Brandon meant by that?

Her hands went clammy and her vision blurred, but she pushed down what she knew was coming back. She could hold on for a bit longer as she'd trained herself to do, but if she weren't careful, she'd reveal too much, too soon.

"What is it you plan to do to help us?" the newest person said, his voice low, demanding.

"You're the Alpha," she said softly, recognizing him once he came closer. "Gideon Brentwood." She turned to Brandon. "You're his brother, and if you were the one who came out to gauge who I was, I take it you're the Omega. And that man who was out here earlier since you all thought I was a threat, was the Enforcer."

Gideon's eyes went gold, and she pressed her lips together, aware she'd probably said too much. "You seem to know a lot about wolves for someone who says they aren't like their father."

The words were a direct affront, but she took them, as was her due. She hadn't been able to stop her father when it had counted, and now she had to pay the price.

"There're stories about all of you and your positions on every screen out there," she said after a moment. "They have some of the hierarchy but not all, and I'm pretty sure they're making half of it up. But there are a few things that are in each and every one, so I figured those had to be close to the truth." She looked at the three men surrounding her and raised her chin once again. "I hadn't spoken to my father for almost ten years before he died. The only reason I know he's dead at all is because I saw it happen live like everyone else did thanks to the satellite feed. Not to mention the fact that his face is plastered all over the place, labeled as a traitor." She let out a breath. "They haven't revealed the fact that he had a daughter yet since he cut me off and hasn't mentioned me. And I, for one, am grateful for that. I'm not the man who tried to harm you—I'm nothing like him. But I want to find a way to help your Pack if I can."

Gideon narrowed his eyes at her for a moment, and she ducked her head. She might be human, but the power in his gaze was so intense that she instinctively knew not to meet it. Prey knew a predator when they saw one.

"My wolf is saying I can trust you," Gideon growled low. "And my wolf *never* says that these days. So I'm going to hear you out, along with the council and some of my wolves. But you won't be stepping into the den." He paused. "It's too dangerous. Do you understand that?"

She didn't even feel a moment of hurt at that statement. She would have been surprised—and a little disappointed—if they'd let her past their wards so easily. She'd only known where the place was since the field they were currently standing in had been the place for not one, but two battles recently.

"Where do you want to meet, then?" she asked.

"The Chambers would be a good place," Parker put in, never letting his gaze fall from her. She did her best not to squirm under his scrutiny.

"I agree," Brandon added. "But blindfold her before she gets there."

"*She* is standing right here," she said, annoyed. "You don't have to talk like I'm not."

"You're lucky we're letting you talk at all," a fourth wolf said. This one was new, and she didn't recognize him.

"Stop scaring her, Mitchell," Brandon said with a sigh. "We're not going to kill you," he said directly to Avery.

"Thanks for clearing that up," she said dryly.

She could tell Parker was trying to hold back a laugh at her words.

"We're trying to figure out what to do with you, so, yeah, we're going to talk like you're not here. Kind of hard to do anything else when you're on our territory," Brandon added.

Though his words made sense in a way, it still grated. "Fine. Blindfold me, I guess. I came here and put my life in your hands anyway. Might as well keep going."

This time, Parker did chuckle. "I think I like you."

She narrowed her eyes at him. "I don't know if I like you," she said honestly.

Parker's smile widened. "Yeah, I definitely like you."

"Freaking wolf," Brandon muttered so low that Avery almost missed it. He pulled something out of his back pocket and held it out to Parker. "Cover her eyes while I get ahold of the others."

Both Gideon and Kameron watched the three of them with curiosity in their gazes before moving back through the wards, apparently satisfied for the time being. Parker stalked toward her—there was no other word for it with the grace in which he moved—and held out the blindfold.

"This is just so we keep our location secret. I promise you, no harm will come to you while you are with us." His voice was low, reassuring. "We aren't the monsters they show us to be."

"I know that," she whispered, for some reason unable to speak any louder when he was so close, so looming. "That's why I'm here."

He studied her face before nodding. "Good." He reached forward and tied the blindfold over her eyes. Darkness surrounded her, but for some reason, maybe because he was there, right by her side, she didn't feel scared.

Then again, maybe she was truly going insane.

He took her hand, and she jumped. "Sorry. I'm going to lead you to one of our vehicles now so we can get to the meeting place." She stopped where she was at those words. "We're not going to kidnap you."

"The whole blindfold thing kind of belies that point," she said with a laugh.

"As long as you don't go kicking and screaming, it probably won't *feel* like a kidnapping." She laughed again at Parker's words and took a step forward. She felt the relief in his grip as she moved, and she knew she had to trust these men. She was here to atone, after all. Running away at the first sign of trouble wouldn't help anyone.

Soon, Avery found herself sitting in a large

room with tables set in a square pattern so everyone faced one another. Every chair had been filled in record time, and Avery had a feeling she was the only human in attendance. A daunting sense that everything was once again out of her control filled her, and she did her best not to panic.

She was just one person with a tiny plan to help. It wasn't much, but for some reason, these wolves had seemed to trust her enough to meet with her. That had to count for something.

"We're here because the moon goddess spoke to me," Gideon said, breaking the silence.

A few others gasped, but Avery didn't say anything. She'd heard of the goddess before, but she didn't know much, other than the fact that she was directly connected with the shifters.

"What did she say?" another man asked. The power bleeding off of him matched Gideon's, and she looked at him again before remembering that this man was the Alpha of the Redwood Pack, Kade.

"She told me that Avery is important," Gideon answered slowly. "I don't know what that means, and you know the goddess likes to speak in riddles—if she speaks at all." He looked at Avery. "But since she spoke to me, we're here to listen to you."

Avery cleared her throat. "Um...will you tell me who

I'm talking to? That way, I don't mess up protocol or something by talking to the wrong wolf?" She truly was out of her depth, and she knew she only had a short leash with the people her father had hurt so deeply.

A very pregnant woman next to Gideon smiled. "I think introductions are in order, as well."

"I think *you* should be behind the wards," Gideon growled.

The woman raised her brows. "*I* think I'm surrounded by some of the strongest wolves of both Packs and I need to be here. The goddess said so."

"The goddess is out of her mind," Gideon growled.

Lightning flashed across the clear sky, and Avery froze—as did the rest of the room.

"No offense," Gideon said quickly before running a hand over his face.

"Schooled by a goddess," Kade said with a laugh. "Good to know she's listening." The Redwood Alpha turned to Avery with a nod. "You already know who I am, don't you?" he asked.

"You're Kade, Alpha of the Redwood Pack," Avery answered immediately.

Kade nodded. "Good. This is my mate, Melanie." The blonde woman next to Kade nodded. "My Heir and son, Finn." Kade gestured toward the man at his side, who looked remarkably like him. "And his mate, Brynn."

"Brynn is also our sister," Gideon added. "This is my mate, Brie."

The pregnant woman waved before putting her hand down over her large stomach.

"Brie is also my niece," Kade added. "We're...complicated."

Avery snorted. *Complicated* probably didn't even begin to cover it.

Gideon continued the introductions. "Kameron is our Enforcer, Mitchell our Beta. You've already met Parker and Brandon. Though Parker is a Redwood, not a Talon."

Her head was beginning to spin at all the names and titles, but she did her best to pay attention.

"And finally, the others are our council," Gideon said. "They are the ones that make sure our two Packs run smoothly as a unit."

He paused and she tried to catch up.

"Gina, Parker, Farah, and Quinn are the Redwoods. Lorenzo, Kimberly, Max, and Leah are the Talons."

Each of the wolves nodded in her direction as they were named, and she let out a breath. There was no way she was going to remember everyone, but that didn't matter for now. She knew who the Alphas were, and they were here to listen to her. Only now, she was afraid that she was going to let them down.

Avery squirmed in her seat. "I don't really know why

the goddess spoke to you about me. I'm just here with a small plan to help. I mean, I figured I'd talk to one of you and see if I could assist on the sidelines. It's not like my plan has any huge merit beyond goodwill."

"Then maybe the goddess wants you here for something other than your plan," Brandon said softly from her side. She couldn't help but feel the heat radiating off him next to her, just as she did with Parker on her other side.

"But I don't have anything other than this little idea. It doesn't make any sense."

"You're in the world of the paranormal, Avery. Not everything makes sense until the rest of the pieces come together." She looked over at Parker as he spoke, aware that the others were staring, as well.

"What plan do you have?" Gideon asked. "Why did you come to see us?"

She put her hands on the table in front of her. "I'm the daughter of a traitor. I know this. I know only part of what he's done to you, but even that part is far too evil to even contemplate. You all know what he did. I'm here in whatever capacity you need me. If it's to show the world that you can work with a human who has the same blood as a monster, so be it. If it's to show that you want nothing to do with me, I can understand that, too. But I'm also a photojournalist. That's my job by trade and passion. I've spent my life going to war-torn countries and trying to show the rest of the world that people need help outside of our borders. I've tried to find peace for those who cannot find it for themselves." She stopped to catch her breath, yet no one spoke, so she continued. "I know it's not much, but I can show the world who you really are. People fear what they do not know, and if they *know* you, at least as much as you'll allow, they'll find that they don't need to be afraid. Or at least they can be less afraid."

Parker reached out and patted her hand, while Brandon did the same to her knee. It wasn't until they both touched her reassuringly that she realized she hadn't been breathing. She finally sucked in more air, her hands going clammy. If she weren't careful, she'd reveal the rest of her reason for being there.

"We tried doing something like that before," Kade added. "And we lost some of our own in the process."

She nodded. "I'm sorry."

"Are we ready to show the world who we are?" Gideon asked quietly, his hand over Brie's on her stomach. "Because, like Kade said, we tried that and it didn't work. They killed us. Our blood is on the field out there right next to your father's. Would it be better for them to fear us? I don't know. But I don't want my child, our future Alpha, to die or live knowing I didn't do what I could to help."

Avery wrung her hands together. "I don't know what

you should do. But I will say that the humans out there watching the screens and whatever news the media can report about you don't know the truth. They see what the media wants them to see, and honestly, I don't know if the reporters know their own message. They say they want a fair fight, that they want the truth, but growling wolves and death pays more than seeing the truth about the atrocities being leveled against you."

"And you think you can help?" Gideon asked, his tone neutral enough that she had no idea what he was thinking.

The only reason she wasn't jumping out of her skin was the fact that Brandon and Parker were on either side of her—stone sentries in the face of uncertainty. She had no idea why she felt safe between them, but she of all people knew not to go against her instincts.

"I only know that it can take just one step. You're probably fighting on twenty sides right now, and that's understandable. I know I'm not the final answer, and I told you that before I began, but I can be *part* of the answer if you'll let me."

The wolves studied her for a moment before Gideon stood up. Her heart thudded in her chest, and once again, the two men on either side of her leaned closer, as if reassuring her that she was safe—at least as safe as she could be as the lone human in a roomful of wolves.

"We'll take your proposal under advisement," Gideon said after a moment.

"And considering we don't have much time to screw around, we'll give you an answer by tomorrow," Kade added.

She let out a relieved breath. They were listening. That had to count for something. At least they hadn't killed her right off like some of the media had said would happen. She hadn't believed that would be the case, but with tension riding high and the fact that her father had been a murdering bastard, she hadn't been a hundred percent sure she'd be safe.

"Thank you for listening," she said softly before standing up. "I know you have countless other things to do, but thank you."

The two Alphas nodded as one, and she wondered if they even knew they'd done that. It was interesting to see how well the two dominant Packs got along in close quarters.

As she began to leave the room, Parker and Brandon followed her. It seemed they would be continuing their roles as her guards. Safeguarding her from danger or saving the wolves from her, she didn't know.

"Do you have a place to stay?" Brandon asked. "From what you said, you don't seem to live around here, and your father lived out near DC. We knew of your father's background from whatever we could dig up during our research, but he did a decent job of hiding your existence from any files we could find."

She tried not to let any of what Brandon said hurt. It wasn't their fault that her father had cut her out of his life. Of course, now that she knew even more about the man, she was actually grateful.

"I rented a motel room in the town closest to the den," she answered. There was no reason to lie since they'd probably have someone follow her back anyway to keep an eye on her. She wouldn't blame them.

"Do you need us to take you there?" Parker asked. "It's not exactly safe around our den anymore."

She shook her head. "No, I'll be fine. No one knows who I am, and since I'm human…" She winced. "Hell. I'm sorry."

"No, you're right," Brandon corrected. "You're human and far safer than any of us. But our enemies don't know how to tell who is shifter or not, so be careful. We'll send word of the Alphas' decision as soon as we know it."

She nodded and took the blindfold from Parker as he held it out. She'd done what she'd come to do, and now she just had to hope it would be enough.

By the time they stopped, and she got out of the car right back where they'd started, darkness was coming, and she knew she needed to get to her safe place soon. She'd pushed away the vision for too long, and if she weren't careful, she'd pass out in the middle of the forest.

"Thank you," she said as she pulled on her pack. "I appreciate it."

"Thank *you*," Brandon said. "You're trying to help us even though you don't know us."

She shrugged. "It's what anyone would do."

"You're wrong about that," Parker said with a shake of his head. "It's going to be dark soon. You'd better get back to where you parked your vehicle."

She gave them both one last searching look, not knowing why she felt such a…connection to them. It didn't make any sense, but it wouldn't matter in the long run. She was the daughter of the man who had tried to kill them.

Nothing more.

Nothing less.

Avery pressed her lips together as she made her way back to her car, aware that she didn't have much time before she blacked out. Her hands were clammy, and sweat rolled down her back.

"Almost there," she breathed, running out of time.

She was so focused on getting to her vehicle, she almost missed the growl. Hair rising on the back of her neck, she turned, only to open her mouth on a soundless scream.

Gold eyes.
Sharp teeth.
Torn flesh.
Searing pain.
Nothing.

CHAPTER 4

PARKER SLID through the wards on his way back into the den, ignoring the pinpricks of sensation along his skin. He ran a hand over the back of his neck. "Something's wrong."

"You mean beyond the fact that no matter what we do, the Packs keep facing the unknown?" Brandon asked, a frown on his face. The other man rubbed his side, and Parker held back a frown. He knew Brandon had healed from the gunshot wound, there wasn't even a scar since their Healer knew what he was doing, but it still had to ache sometimes. He hated that he'd been too slow to help him when it had mattered.

He pushed those thoughts from his head, focusing on what mattered now and not what he couldn't change.

"No, not that. I mean, yeah, that too, but something about what we just left. I can't place it, but..."

Brandon stopped in his tracks, and Parker did the same, his wolf rising slightly to the surface. "We shouldn't have left her on her own in the dark."

Parker looked up at the darkening clouds and cursed. "A storm's coming in, making it feel later than it is. It wasn't that bad when we left her..."

"But that was only a few minutes ago, and now it's worse. Shit." Brandon turned on his heel. "Let's just make sure she made it back to her car alone. We shouldn't have let her leave like that anyway."

"Because she should be safe," Parker bit out as he once again slid through the wards. Magic sliced over him, tugging at his wolf. Since he wasn't a Talon, going through the wards hurt more than if he'd been going through the Redwood's. Because he was a guest and under the Alpha's invitation, he could go back and forth without a Talon member at his side, but it still hurt like hell.

"Her car was only like fifty feet away behind the copse of trees," Brandon muttered. "Still..."

"Still, we shouldn't have just let her go alone." Parker shook his head, annoyed with himself for thinking that anyone could be safe anymore. Avery had shown up at the den *because* of their lack of security, and yet he and

Brandon hadn't made sure she made it to her vehicle safely.

If it weren't for the fact that his head was in a thousand different places, he might have actually done what he was supposed to do, instead of going half-assed. But between what was going on inside his body, the fact that he was in a new and unfamiliar den yet again, and his weird attraction to not only Brandon but also Avery, it was all a little too much for him.

As soon as he and Brandon made it completely through the wards, Parker knew something had gone terribly wrong. The two sentries on duty turned, their wolves in their gazes.

"Blood," the one closest snarled. "It just hit the wind."

Parker cursed.

"We're on it. Notify Gideon," Brandon bit out as he started to run to where Avery had gone off. Parker followed, his wolf reared up fully now.

At that moment, it didn't matter that he was growing weaker with each passing day. It didn't matter that something was terribly wrong with his wolf and the blood in his veins. It didn't even matter that the man by his side—the man who had a chip on his shoulder for some reason—was in a similar boat as Parker regarding health. They each had secrets, each was growing weak for a reason beyond what Parker could comprehend.

But none of it mattered right then.

Not when blood filled the air, and the woman who had been in his charge was in danger.

They made it past a group of trees, and a growl ripped from his throat. An unknown sandy-colored wolf loomed over Avery's prone body, blood on his muzzle and mud splattered in his tangled fur. The wolf had turned as soon as Brandon and Parker came into view, so it faced them as it stood over Avery's still form.

From what Parker could see, bite marks covered her body, torn open flesh a macabre display as a tableau of blood pooled beneath her. He could still scent life on her, but whatever she had left was fading fast. If they didn't get her to an Alpha soon, she'd die.

And because he *knew* she was so close to death, there was only one other option—she had to change.

To become shifter.

Fuck.

But first, Parker and Brandon needed to take care of the piece of shit who had *dared* to hurt an innocent woman. Because she was innocent, damn it. No matter what her father had done, *she* had had nothing to do with it.

Curious statement coming from you, he thought to himself and pushed that out of his mind. There was no time for that now—not ever.

"You're fucking dead," Parker growled. "Do you understand that? You know the laws. You *never* change an unwilling, and *never* without an Alpha present. Your life is forfeit."

The wolf growled at them, his back arched.

"Look at his eyes," Brandon said softly. "There's something wrong."

Parker met the gold eyes of the rogue wolf and let out a curse. "He's gone truly rogue. Someone did a number on him, but fuck, there's nothing we can do right now for him. Not without losing Avery in the process."

"Damn it," Brandon growled.

"Go," Parker ordered, his fangs elongating and his claws poking out from his fingertips. It took too long to change fully, but at his power level, he could at least partially shift so he'd have a better chance of fighting this wolf. Since the other shifter had gone rogue, it would fight as if it had nothing to lose—making it all the more dangerous. "Get Avery."

Brandon growled low. "On it."

Then they *moved*.

Brandon darted to the right as Parker went head-on. The other wolf ignored Brandon, taking in the larger of the two as the threat. Little did this wolf know that Brandon could fight just as hard as Parker, but that didn't matter now. Parker just had to get this wolf off of Avery's body so that Brandon had a way of getting her to Gideon to save her.

The wolf lowered his head as if to bite Avery again, and Parker slashed out, his claws raking along the sandy wolf's hide. The rogue howled, leaping toward Parker in the next breath. Parker moved to the side, growling as he slid his claws along the wolf's flank once more.

The rogue turned back to attack, and Parker moved so his back was to Avery and Brandon, protecting them from whatever this other wolf might do. As he turned, out of the corner of his eye, he could see Brandon assessing Avery's wounds, covering her body with his in the process. Parker wasn't sure if they should even move her, but they might not have a choice if he didn't take this wolf down soon.

The only problem was, he had a feeling this wolf was far stronger than he'd planned for. Whatever had made it go rogue must have been horrific, because he had to have been high in the power structure within his Pack.

Meaning if Parker weren't careful, he might not be able to come out of this unscathed, especially in his weakened state.

To hell with that.

His wolf panted at the surface, much more tired than it should have been with such little energy spent. He cursed, using whatever power he had left to lunge. The wolf in front of him jumped, as well, but Parker—thankfully—was slightly faster. He wrapped his arm around the wolf's neck and used his other arm to keep its body in place. With one twist, he snapped its neck, knowing that the wolf had been beyond saving.

And he hadn't missed the plea hidden deep within the rogue's eyes.

It was dead before it had even bitten Avery the first time and it knew it.

Parker let the wolf slide to the ground as he fought to catch his breath. His body shook, and he bent over, bile filling his throat. Holy fuck. Whatever illness had taken hold and weakened him when he touched that damn box back with the elders of the European Pack was truly killing him. He shouldn't be out of breath and on the verge of throwing up after one small fight.

He was even weaker now than he had been on the battlefield against Montag. The progression of whatever was killing him was speeding up, and Parker knew he only had so much time before he lost it all.

He let out a breath at the sound of people running toward him and stood up, wiping his face. He couldn't show them weakness, not now, not ever. And he was well aware that Brandon was still behind him, watching everything.

Well, Parker had already seen Brandon weak; turnabout was fair play, after all.

He pushed aside thoughts of his wolf and his weakening dominance and turned back to where Avery lay in Brandon's arms.

"Shit." He moved the few steps that separated them and fell to his knees. "She's not going to make it."

Brandon's eyes were wild, blue rimmed with gold. Fierce. "I can't stop the bleeding," he croaked. "And if I move her, I might tear whatever's not already torn away."

"You need to move her anyway," Gideon growled as he ran toward them. "That wolf was almost an Alpha, meaning he'd have had enough strength in him for the change to take hold."

Only an Alpha or a wolf almost as strong as one could bring the change forward. That was why it was so hard to make wolves. A weaker wolf could bite someone, but the human would either bleed out or die from infection—if they couldn't somehow find the will to survive. Sometimes, if they were mates chosen by the goddess, by fate, they could bring on the change, but that was rare.

"What does that mean?" Parker asked, his hands over some of the worst wounds. Blood seeped through his fingers, and his wolf howled. Avery didn't deserve this. *No one* deserved this.

"It means she'll change if we can get her back through

the wards," Gideon growled. "Get her up now, Brandon. I can't fucking help her outside of the damn wards with the satellites watching. We only have so many secrets left." His words were so low that Parker knew no one but the three of them would have been able to hear. "We have to protect our people *and* Avery."

Parker stood up at the same time as Brandon, Avery between them. Without words, he helped roll her into Brandon's arms firmly before the other wolf took off running, Gideon on his heels. Parker looked down at the blood on his hands and tried to focus.

"Come on, Parker," Mitchell growled. Parker had been aware that the other wolf had shown up with Gideon, but his attention had been on Avery and not the Beta of the Talon Pack. "We have to go, before someone shows up. My men are moving Avery's car, and I've got the rogue. But we need to get behind the wards and regroup."

Parker nodded and took off beside Mitchell. The other man held the rogue to his chest, the anger radiating off of him so thick that Parker could feel it, and he wasn't even a damn Omega. Someone had sent this wolf after Avery. Either that, or they'd sent him to the den for another reason, and Parker needed to know what that was. From the look in the wolf's eyes before he died, Parker had a feeling the dead man had wanted no part in whatever had gone on.

Something big was coming; Parker could feel it; only he had no idea what it was.

For the third time that day, Parker slid through the Talon wards, his skin raw from the onslaught of magic. Others were scrambling around him, doing his or her duty for the Pack, but Parker could only follow Brandon's scent trail, needing to make sure they could save Avery. His wolf was silent during it all, which worried him, but he had to focus on what mattered right then, and that was the life of an innocent woman who'd only wanted to help those she'd never even met.

He stormed through the infirmary doors, aware that Mitchell had veered off at some point with the dead rogue in his arms. Parker's hands shook as he made his way to the room where they'd set Avery down, praying that she'd find a way to fight.

"Is she going to make it?" Parker bit out.

Walker, the Talon Healer, looked up at that moment, his hands hovering over the deepest wounds on Avery's body. "I don't know."

Walker turned back and started working on her wounds alongside Leah, a witch and a healer in her own right. They weren't using magic since Avery wasn't connected to the Pack, but they were at least trying to do what they could medically.

Gideon cursed. "The wolf that bit her smelled of Pack, but I don't know which one."

"He was an Aspen Pack member," Parker growled. Everyone turned to him, and he lifted a lip, baring fang. "I know all of the scents now that I've visited them. He smelled faintly of Aspen, but it had been a long time since he'd been to the den."

"He could have been held somewhere else before he came out here," Brandon put in. "There was just a manic energy seeping off him. So much that I couldn't tell anything about what he was truly feeling. We don't have issues with the Aspens, do we?"

Gideon blew out a breath. "They're one of the more insular Packs, so we might not have beef with them directly, but they might hate us for the Unveiling. Lots of Packs blame us, even if they don't say it. It doesn't matter at this exact moment, though because I'm going to have to bring her into the Pack if we want Walker to save her."

"It's going to hurt her more," Parker said on a growl. "Because right now, whatever change might happen would make her Aspen."

Leah cursed under her breath, blood covering her hands, and Parker did his best not to move to help her. He only had basic first aid training, and he would only be in the way at this point.

Gideon shook his head. "Not necessarily. If the Alpha doesn't automatically trust those high in his hierarchy to bring in another wolf, then the connection won't come. It's not an exact science. The thing is, if we bring her into the Talons, we bring whatever she has burdening her, as well. We're still trying to untangle the ramifications from the last time we brought an unknown into the Pack bonds, and my wolf is telling me that doing this will add to that. She didn't ask for this. We don't know if she'd have wanted to become a wolf at all, and yet she might not have a choice unless we snap her neck right now. So either we watch and see what happens, trying to save her the human way, or we bring her into the Pack and be sure that she'll live. Only as a wolf rather than the human she thought she'd die as." He cursed. "The world can already guess how we're made, but now, they'll *know*."

"So you'd rather we let her die?" Brandon spat.

Gideon growled, *power* radiating off him. "I'm bringing her in. I can't watch her die, but we also need to protect our people. I'm Alpha, damn it. I have a duty."

"Brandon and I will take care of her," Parker said without thinking.

Brandon's gaze darted to his, and the others gave him

curious looks. He honestly didn't know why he'd said that, but he *knew* the words were meant to come from him.

"We'll protect her," Brandon said slowly. "And ensure she's not a threat to the Pack."

Gideon looked between the two of them once more before using his claw to slash a cut along his palm. The Alpha pressed his now bloody hand over one of the bite marks and squeezed. Though Avery had been passed out and motionless this entire time, her entire body jerked at the contact. Parker growled, taking a step forward without thinking, but it was Brandon who held him back. The other man wrapped an arm around Parker's stomach and held him there, his back to Avery but his gaze on Parker.

"We need to let him do this," Brandon whispered. Again, their voices were so low that not even the Alpha in the room could have heard.

"We should have been there." Parker's voice was raw, guttural, and he hated himself more in that moment than he had when he'd realized that something was wrong when he stepped through the wards. If he and Brandon hadn't let her go off on her own, Avery might not have been attacked as she was.

Or she could have been attacked later at her motel if she were the true target.

They might not ever know, but Parker would forever blame himself for the agonizing pain she was in at that moment. And each time Gideon cut himself before closing his hand over another wound, Parker hated himself even more.

He'd done this.

He and Brandon.

And now, Avery would pay the price.

"It's done," Gideon growled. "She's Pack. Talon."

"She's in so much pain," Brandon gasped, and Parker moved to hold the other man up. "And not just from what happened on that field."

Walker looked up at that moment, his eyes glassy. "Yes, it's something *more*."

"Goddess help us for what we've done." Gideon's plea radiated through them all, and Parker bowed his head.

They'd saved Avery's life, but at what cost?

"It'll be a few hours at least," Walker said after a moment. "Come back in a little while, but give me some time to work."

Parker never truly understood how Healers worked within a Pack since it was different for each of them, but he did know that a lot of their work was personal. And though he'd just told the others he would protect Avery, he knew he needed to give Walker privacy to Heal what he could.

Each change was different. Each Healer was different. Each Alpha…different.

Parker wasn't a Talon member, but watching how the Talons worked, he knew that their Pack did everything in their power to ensure their Pack's safety, even when the cards were stacked against them.

Brandon tugged on his shirt, and Parker followed the other man to one of the other rooms without saying a word. Leah and Gideon both left, as well, and Parker could scent their mates waiting on the other side of the building. He craved a mating bond of his own, and it had nothing to do with the fact that a bond would save his life.

He wanted someone to hold, to hold him when he couldn't take the pressures of this war or his life anymore. Yet, he had no one.

"We need to clean off the blood," Brandon said after a moment. "There are two big sinks here."

Parker shook his head, clearing his thoughts. "Okay." He wasn't sure he had much more in him right then to say anything more.

They cleaned off their arms and necks, standing side-by-side in silence. They both needed a change of clothes, but he figured that wouldn't be happening until they made it back to the house. And that probably wouldn't happen until after Avery woke.

He'd been in worse positions in his life. A little dried blood wasn't going to kill him.

"We shouldn't have left her there," Brandon bit out

after a moment.

Parker cleared his throat. "I know. It's our fault."

"Damn straight, it is. We fucking *left* her to that rogue. Didn't even scent the bastard until we were right on top of him. She's lying there dying, maybe becoming a shifter and having her entire life changed without her consent, and we're the ones responsible."

Parker turned on Brandon, his wolf waking up again, anger filling him. "Yeah, I get it. But don't fucking yell at me. Got it? There's nothing we can do now except make sure Avery knows she's not alone."

Brandon snorted. "Yeah, like's she's going to want to be near us when she wakes up and realizes what happened. You're not an Omega, not Pack. You can't feel what I do, Parker. She's *hurting*. She's always been alone, always frightened. And yet we did nothing about it."

Parker threw up his hands. "We don't know anything about her, damn it. We did what we were supposed to do and brought her back to the meeting place. We didn't invite her into the wards or give her a damn cup of tea because *we don't know her*. She could still be an enemy for all we know."

Brandon raised his chin. "An enemy we brought into the Talons. Not the Redwoods. So you wouldn't understand."

Parker growled. "You think I don't understand

enemies? That I don't understand traitors within a Pack? Do you not know what I came from? What monster forced a mating on my mother? He used dark magic to make sure she got pregnant. You remember that part in the history lessons? She had to run from *this* Pack because your dad, your former *Alpha,* couldn't stand the sight of her anymore and was too chickenshit to do anything about the Centrals. So my mom, a woman you *knew,* ran away with her brother, an outcast from the Pack. And then I was born with no Pack, no family beyond the two people who had sacrificed everything for me. So don't tell me I don't understand, Brandon. The blood in my veins is proof enough."

Brandon sighed, reaching out for Parker at the same instant. Parker didn't move back as Brandon gripped his arm, keeping him steady. He just didn't have much left these days to fight.

"I knew Lexi and Logan. We all did. But we also couldn't do anything about it. We were being tortured daily, and our Pack was dying because of the older generation. I didn't even know that she'd been cut from the Pack because I wasn't the Omega back then. I didn't know anything about it until it was too late." The other man paused, and Parker's breath finally settled. "I'm sorry for saying what I did. I'm just pissed off, and you're the only one here for me to lash out at."

Parker let out a breath. "Same. It's just all a little too much, you know?"

Brandon nodded, his gaze resting on Parker's lips. "I know." Then the other man leaned in, and Parker didn't move away, no, he moved *forward*.

Brandon's lips were soft yet strong, the kiss tentative, as if neither was sure why they were doing this. Parker closed his eyes, letting the taste of the other man settle on his tongue.

Then the reality of what was going on hit him, and Parker pulled away, clenching his fists at his sides.

"Shit. This is not the time for this."

Brandon's breathing was just as ragged as his. "There's never going to be a time with the way things are going."

Parker met Brandon's gaze, hurt and indecision running through his body. "I need a mate, Brandon. Not a fuck. And you're not my mate. This can't happen again."

And with that, he pushed past Brandon, knocking the other man back, and stormed out of the building. He was going to fucking lose it if he weren't careful, and yet…and yet, he couldn't get Brandon's taste out of his mind.

He'd just made a mistake, and if he weren't careful, he'd do it again.

Soon.

CHAPTER 5

AGONY SEARED OVER HIS SKIN, and a scream ripped from Brandon's throat. He rolled to the side, trying to get away from the animal's fangs, but it was too late. It bit into his side, tearing the flesh away from him. He held up his arms as it went for his face, and he screamed again, the beast's teeth digging in.

The wolf—he could clearly see it was a wolf now—left him on the ground, bleeding and in pain and jumped at Brandon's two brothers. Shock covered their faces as they tried to fight off the wolf, but it was too late. Soon, the three of them lay on the ground, blood covering them as they each tried to catch their breath.

The wolf in front of them blinked, its eyes full of remorse as if it had just come back to itself rather than the monster it had become.

Brandon looked at his two brothers again, wondering why Walker and Kameron were wearing such different clothing and why things felt...*off*.

Pain seared his side once more, and he woke up.

Woke up.

Brandon lifted a shaky hand to his face and wiped off some of the sweat. Hell. That had all been a nightmare. Yet it had been the most vivid dream he'd ever experienced. It felt as if it were a memory, not something he'd just made up. But that couldn't be the case.

For one, he had more than two brothers. He just happened to be triplets with Kameron and Walker. Plus, he'd never been in a fight like that alongside the two of them. He'd felt weaker during the dream, almost human. None of them had been wearing the right clothes, and even the forest around them had looked off...younger, maybe.

Plus, he had a feeling the wolf attacking them had been trying to change them yet hadn't known how. That made no sense, though because he and his brothers had been *born* and not *made*.

Brandon pressed his head back into his pillow and tried to shove the weird dream from his mind. Watching Avery almost die and then having Gideon bring her into the Pack with freshly made bonds must have triggered the weird dream. As for why Walker and Kameron had been in it, well, he'd always felt more of a connection to them than the others in his family. They may be fraternal triplets, and at their ages, even the two to six-year age differences between them all didn't mean much, but he'd shared a womb with Kameron and Walker.

It counted for something, even if he couldn't explain it.

But then again, he was the Omega of the Talon Pack, there were lots of things he just *knew* and couldn't explain.

Brandon once again ran a hand over his face. His body had broken out in a clammy sweat, and his vision kept blurring. Hell, he felt like he did whenever the wards buckled, and he knew that wasn't good. Whatever had caused that dream had truly fucked with him.

He felt as if someone had hung him up and wrung him dry and yet he hadn't actually been in a fight the night before. It had been Parker doing all the heavy lifting while Brandon had stood guard over Avery. It had made sense at the time since Parker was slightly more dominant than he was, as well as a better fighter. But then Brandon had seen how weak the other man had looked afterward. He hadn't mentioned it and hadn't said anything to the others, but Brandon was worried.

Both of them were walking a fine line, and yet he wasn't sure what they were going to do about it.

Just like he wasn't sure what they were going to do about that kiss.

Shit. He hadn't meant to kiss Parker like that. He hadn't meant to kiss him *at all*. Ever. Just because his dick happened to want the other guy, didn't mean he did. Both he and Parker were looking for their mates, and it was clear now that they weren't it for each other.

The moon goddess always showed their wolves who their potential mates were. That's how it had *always* worked.

And nothing had happened between the two of them that indicated they could be mates. Meaning that kiss had just been in the heat of the moment, and since neither of them wanted a fuck—as Parker had put it—there was no use going down that road.

He rubbed his hand over his heart. Only...only something was different. He could remember the first time he'd seen Parker after he'd come back to the country, the first time they'd been near each other in years. There had been...something there. Something he couldn't quite understand, but then it had vanished as quickly as it had appeared.

Brandon forced himself into a sitting position, ignoring the aches and pains throughout his body. There was something different with the Pack bonds. He'd noticed it for the first time when Shane had come into the

Pack. Shane hadn't been changed the normal way because of something General Montag had done to him, and because of that, Shane wasn't exactly a normal shifter. When they'd introduced that into the Pack, the bonds between each of them had altered slightly.

This wasn't the first time something like this had happened, of course. The Redwoods had done something similar, but nothing to this extent from what he could glean from their bonds. And even with his former Alpha and the hierarchy, they'd forsaken their duties for so long that the moon goddess had begun to shun them—not even allowing them to have an Omega to help heal their emotional wounds. He'd never blamed her for that decision, not when he knew that any Omega at that point in time would have died under the onslaught of betrayal brought on by their former Alpha.

But for some reason, Brandon had a feeling that something far deeper than Pack bonds had been changed. There were more bonds than just those between the hierarchy—the Alpha, Heir, Omega and so on—and the rest of the Pack. There were also *mating* bonds.

He closed his eyes, praying he was wrong.

Because if something had altered the mating bonds, or rather, how mating bonds were made, then the entire basis for how shifters found their other halves would be forever changed.

He shook his head and got out of bed. He was probably just overreacting because of the dream. That and Avery and Parker, of course. He had far too much on his plate, and was now trying to make things worse by overthinking.

He strode naked to the bathroom so he could jump in the shower and wash off the sweat from his dream. His body still ached, but he had things to do today. While he wanted to go straight to Avery and check in on her, since she'd been unconscious the last time he'd seen her, he had to check in with Brie for their weekly visits. Since she was pregnant with her first child and a submissive at that, she needed a little extra care right then. Gideon was protective as hell, and Brandon knew that sometimes Brie just needed time to breathe. Since he was the Omega, it was his duty, and privilege in this case, to help.

He quickly took a shower and got dressed so he wouldn't be late. He'd slept past his alarm again, and knew he'd have to grab a protein bar on the way out. Knowing Brie, she'd have a baked good of some sort for him to munch on, as well.

He ran into Parker in the hallway and froze. He hadn't seen the other man since the kiss and wasn't sure what to say. He wasn't about to apologize, but acting like nothing had happened didn't seem right either.

"I'm off to see Avery and check if she's awake yet," Parker said instead of *good morning*.

Brandon nodded. "I'll be by after I check in on Brie."

Parker's eyes widened. "Is she okay?"

"Yes, but we do weekly meetings to check in on each other and the Pack. I'm sure your Omega does the same with the pregnant women in your Pack."

Parker visibly relaxed. "Yeah, Drake does. Maddox still goes around with him too most times since he still feels such a strong connection to us all."

Brandon couldn't help but smile. "You're lucky you have so many Pack members who want to help."

Parker swallowed hard. "I guess."

Brandon let out a breath. "I guess I'll see you when I get to the infirmary."

Parker nodded. "I don't plan on leaving her side if I can help it."

"I'll be there soon." He turned and walked away at that, hating the awkwardness between the two of them. Hell, they'd always had this weirdness, but now, it was worse. It didn't help that they were forced to live together thanks to his meddling Alpha, either.

The feeling in the den was tense as usual, and he did his best to untangle some of the worst parts as he made his way to Gideon and Brie's. His wolf did a lot of it without

Brandon's help since it was so instinctual, but sometimes, the threads of emotions needed extra care.

Brie opened the door before he could knock, and he couldn't help but smile at her. She'd always been soft and beautiful, a fierce submissive who protected her dominants even if they didn't think they needed protecting. Now, she was even more radiant and about as big as a house.

Not that he'd mention the last part to her or Gideon. Ever.

"Brandon," she said with a smile. "Gideon just left to talk with Kameron and Mitchell about the rogue, but I'm glad you're here and didn't have to cancel."

Brandon leaned down and pressed a soft kiss to her cheek. He didn't hold her close in a hug anymore since Gideon was more territorial than usual given her advanced pregnancy, but he could at least get away with bussing her on the cheek. And Brie needed touch, even with her big, bad Alpha of a mate growling next to her.

"Should you be standing?" he asked, sidestepping the rogue conversation for now. He'd help on that front if they asked, but he knew his role in the Pack, and Brie was the main focus, at least for this hour.

She rolled her eyes, exasperation evident on her face. "You sound like Gideon now."

Brandon smiled despite his rough morning and led

her into the living room where she'd set out fresh pastries and homemade orange juice. If he wasn't afraid of Gideon ripping his face off for doing so, he'd have been jealous at how much Brie took care of what was hers. Gideon was a tad possessive with his pregnant mate.

"I'd be more afraid if it were Walker who told you to get off your feet, not Gideon. He always says that."

She maneuvered herself to the couch, and he didn't help her. She might be a submissive wolf, but she still had fangs.

"He's all broody and won't let me help him with anything." She gestured toward the food. "Eat. Though I didn't make it as he told me to sit down on my pretty ass this morning."

Brandon choked on the pastry he'd just put in his mouth. "So did Gideon bake this?"

Brie narrowed her eyes. "Is it burned?" They both let out a soft laugh. "Of course, he didn't do this. He can cook, but he can't bake. Mom sent these over from the Redwood den."

Brandon leaned back on the couch and smiled, his wolf content in Brie's presence. He might be the Omega, but he was still a dominant wolf. Being around someone of Brie's power and inner strength soothed him as much as his ties to her would soothe her wolf.

"I forgot your mom runs the bakery within the den."

Brie smiled widely as she ran her fingers over the swell of her belly. "I learned to bake at her side in that place. It's been open for as long as my mom and dad have been mated. I've been thinking about opening one here, but I just don't think I'll be able to find the time. I know we're in the middle of a hundred things that are far more important, and a bakery doesn't seem like much of a need. But, sometimes, we need the domestic side of life to remember what we're fighting for."

Brandon frowned, thinking. "There are wolves in the den that usually live outside during times of peace. They had to give up their jobs and homes in some cases because they weren't safe where they were. I know some are trying to fit in, but not all are doing it as well as they'd like. You should talk to Mitchell. He might know of a few that could help you get things going, or at least feel like they're needed."

Brie's eyes lightened. "Mitchell would know exactly who I need."

"He's the Beta. It's his duty. And I think his wolf needs to work on something like that instead of death and war."

They were both quiet for a moment, aware that no matter how hard they tried to worry about den matters, the outside world would always be looming around them.

"Are you going to tell me what's going on between you and Parker?"

He schooled his features, annoyed with himself that he'd forgotten how perceptive this submissive wolf was. "What do you mean?"

Sadness lingered in her eyes for a bare moment before she let out a soft sigh. "If that's the way you want to play it, I understand. But I have a feeling it's not only Parker your wolf is confused about."

Brandon didn't say anything in response, his silence enough of an answer for her it seemed. He stayed with Brie for another hour, knowing they both needed the time together so they could settle. They were only two members of the Pack, but two of the pivotal members in terms of its health. With Gideon's wolf in constant demand, his brother and Alpha needed his mate as well as the rest of his hierarchy to be healthy and intact. Only Brandon wasn't sure any of them could be truly whole anymore.

He pushed those thoughts from his mind and made his way to the infirmary after leaving Brie. His wolf came to the forefront as he walked, surprising him. Not because his wolf was there, considering that with his powers, his wolf was *always* working on some thread of emotion, but because his wolf seemed to truly care about what happened to Avery.

Hell, *Brandon* cared about what happened to Avery, and he knew it wasn't only because she'd been under his care when she left him and Parker, only to be attacked by a stranger. He wasn't sure what to make of it, but he knew he'd have to figure it out soon. Between dealing with Parker and now Avery, his head hurt, and he hadn't even spoken to them yet.

And he sure hadn't dealt with that *kiss*.

He nodded at Walker as he walked through the infirmary doors but didn't stop to say hello. If his triplet needed him, Walker would call on him. The Brentwood clan might be secretive beyond measure most of the time, but they were slowly learning to rely on one another.

Avery lay on her bed, pale but almost fully healed. Thanks to the shifter DNA now running through her veins, she wouldn't even end up with a scar from the attack unless somehow a witch's magic or a special salt were rubbed on the wounds. Those two things were the only ways he knew of for a shifter to scar, and he thanked the goddess that neither of them had been used on Avery.

She'd been hurt enough from the attack, and being forced to look at a daily reminder would be too much. Of course, she would now share her body with the soul of a wolf and would have to deal with the aggression that came in waves from that. He wasn't sure where she'd lie within the hierarchy—dominant, maternal, submissive, or somewhere in between—as their human forms and personalities didn't always mesh with what their wolves needed. There were shy dominants, and outgoing submissives like Brie, but those weren't the norm.

None of that mattered at the moment, though.

Avery had to be strong enough to survive her first full moon...and she didn't have a lot of time to heal beforehand.

"Brandon."

At the sound of her ragged, soft voice, he looked up and focused on her face. She was pale, fear within her eyes, but *alive*. He had to focus on that. Anything else would just make him insane.

The fragile bond that lay between them, which told him that she was Pack to his Omega, burned—newly made and tenuous at best.

Parker cleared his throat from the bedside, and Brandon finally looked over at the man whom he'd done his best not to think about all day.

Why was this so awkward?

"I brought sandwiches and soup from the house," the other man said softly. "I didn't know when you'd show up, but I brought some for you, too."

"Walker said I could eat whatever I want and even get out of the infirmary and into...well, I don't know where,"

Avery said softly. "But I don't have to sleep here after tonight for what it's worth."

"You can stay with us," Brandon blurted. He hadn't known he was going to say that until it was already out of his mouth, but now that the words were out there, he couldn't take them back. And, honestly, he wasn't sure he wanted to.

Parker gave him an odd look as if assessing him before nodding. "There's enough room," the other man said after a moment.

Avery's eyes were wide. "I don't even know you. Why would I move in with you? Hell, everything's moving too fast. I feel like I'm two steps behind and never going to catch up."

The worry and fear that bled off her in waves slammed into him, and Brandon did what he'd been born to do and took care of them. He wrapped himself around the emotional cords and brought them into himself, his wolf taking care of the rest by fading them into the complicated network of bonds he held for the Pack. His own psyche would absorb whatever came at him, but he wouldn't show that he felt what the others did. Not always.

Avery's eyes widened. "You're taking my pain," she whispered. "Stop it. I need that so I can remember that this isn't what I signed up for. And you shouldn't hurt yourself because I'm hurting."

Brandon stopped and moved to sit beside her bed. "It's my duty."

"I don't want to *be* your duty."

Tension filled the room, and Brandon shifted on his seat.

"Let's all get something to eat," Parker said, ever the mediator. "Full bellies will help us think."

Brandon took the offered sandwich and bit in, letting the mustard and roast beef pull him out of his mood. "I wasn't aware I had roast beef in the fridge at home."

Parker grinned. "Leah stopped by with groceries since she said you'd probably only have protein shakes. She wasn't wrong." He met Brandon's eyes, studying him. "Though I don't think she knows *why* you only drink those these days," he whispered.

"Will you tell me why?" Avery asked, and Brandon pulled away from Parker to look at her. Why was it that he couldn't focus with either of them near? And, hell, put the two of them together, and he almost lost control fully.

Brandon didn't answer her, but he wasn't sure she wanted an answer right then. She played with her soup, her brows furrowed.

"I'm a wolf." Her words contained so much confusion,

so much hollow pain, he wasn't sure his own wolf could handle the onslaught.

Brandon set down the rest of his meal, not in the mood to eat anymore.

"Yes," he answered, though her words hadn't been a question. "Someone not of our Pack attacked you outside our home, and now you'll shift."

"We couldn't let you die," Parker added, his words rough. "Maybe we should have," he said after a moment.

Brandon growled as Avery let out an involuntary gasp.

The other man held up his hands. "Shit. I didn't mean it like *that*. I meant we took the choice out of your hands. Gideon had to bring you into the Talons so Walker could Heal you enough that you'd be able to survive your wounds. Not all those who are attacked and bitten to near death survive, but *you* did."

And she wasn't out of the woods yet, though he wouldn't say that. Walker would have already told her when she'd woken up, as his brother never hid the details of what would come next. But Brandon didn't want to throw that in her face again.

Avery studied her hands, and Brandon did the only thing he could at that moment—he reached out and put one of his hands on hers. The connection was immediate, warmth and a shocking intensity he couldn't quite name shooting through him. Avery's gaze flashed to his before going to Parker as the other man gripped her other hand.

Brandon swallowed hard, the circuit the three of them made almost overwhelming.

Yet his wolf refused to tell him if they were potential mates. How could this be? He'd *never* felt anything like this, and yet he was in the dark.

Something had happened to the mating bonds, and he needed to figure out what that was. But before he did, he needed to ensure that Avery was okay.

"The full moon is in two days," Brandon said softly, bringing Avery's gaze back to his. He could find peace in those eyes, he knew, if he only looked long enough—if she only gave him enough time.

"You'll change then," Parker added. "There's no way around it. Are you ready for that?"

She met both of their gazes. "I don't have a choice, do I?"

Brandon frowned. "You don't." Anger boiled in his veins once more. "Not anymore. A wolf not of ours made that choice for you, and we manifested it into being so you would breathe again."

Avery looked down at their clasped hands, concentration on the parts of her face he could see. "I said I would help you...help your people, your Packs. Now, I guess I will help myself, as well."

At her words, Brandon's wolf howled in respect, and his gaze shot up to meet Parker's. The other man's eyes glowed gold, and their wolves reached out as if needing one another for a purpose Brandon had yet to name.

This woman, this *wolf to-be*, was so damned strong. Stronger than the two others in this room, and he had a feeling she didn't even know it.

No matter what happened next, what happened between the three of them, he knew Avery would go on to do great things. She was Pack now, one of them.

She was wolf.

And a small part of him whispered that one day soon...she might be *his*.

CHAPTER 6

AVERY HAD ALWAYS BEEN good at keeping secrets. It was one of the things she'd learned to do as a child, barely able to write sentences. She'd known from a young age that the moment her father knew the truth about her, he'd find a way to silence her the same way he'd ended her mother's life.

So she'd never spoken aloud who she was, what she could do.

Soon, she knew she wouldn't be able to hold it back any longer. Because the new Pack threads were slowly weaving their way around her soul, and there would be no hiding what lay beneath her shields once the Alpha and his family understood what they'd brought into their Pack.

She wasn't dangerous, but she wasn't normal either.

She'd known that the moment she spoke to the

Talons, her life would be forever altered. She'd known that one day, she would become wolf and run on four paws. She'd share her soul with another being and learn to become something that had once only lived in fairy tale books and the nightmares of those who didn't understand.

She'd *seen* it.

Yet she hadn't known *how* it would happen.

Nor had she known *why* she'd seen the vision. She'd never once seen her own future when her mind lost control and she was forced to see what hadn't yet come to pass.

But for some reason, *this* vision had come to her, and she'd known it was more important than any of the others she'd had.

Now, she stood under the full moon, the wind in her hair, and fear almost too much to deal with. But the moon's rays covered her like a well worn blanket and she felt like she could breathe again. Maybe. Parker stood by her side, his hand on hers, and she tried not to lean into his touch like she wanted to. Before the attack, she'd been attracted to not only Parker but Brandon, as well. And now, whatever was going on between the three of them only seemed to intensify.

Her senses were overwhelmed by the scent of them, of the trees, the sky, the birds. Everything seemed so loud and bright, and she couldn't quite focus. Maybe she'd be able to deal over time, but right now, it was all too much.

"Gideon and the others are right beyond those trees," Parker explained after a moment. "While normally you'd want someone connected to the Pack near you for your first shift, I figured you might like a little privacy. As you know, Brandon wanted to be here, as well, but he…well, he won't be shifting tonight with us."

There was more to what he was saying—or not saying—but she pressed her lips together and nodded. How had she ended up in this clearing with him? One minute, she'd been walking to her car after meeting with some of the most powerful wolves in the area, and the next, she was in the woods, about to get naked and change into a wolf.

How did things like this happen in real life? It didn't make any sense.

But there was no use trying to fix things what couldn't be fixed. She just had to move forward and try to figure it all out. One step at a time.

"What's going to happen again?" They'd told her in the infirmary since she still hadn't had the courage to figure out where she was staying yet, but she needed to hear it again. Hell, she'd hear it another hundred times if it meant that she might finally understand it.

Parker put his hands on her shoulders, and she calmed. He'd said that he wasn't part of the Talons, so there was no connection between them; so then why could he calm her by just his touch?

Because maybe it was something more than a Pack need.

She pushed that thought from her head.

"When you are ready, we'll each strip so we don't tear our clothes. Unlike some movies, we don't tear right through them, and we could end up getting stuck if we're not careful. And they don't disintegrate, so we'll have to deal with them anyway. Then you'll get on all fours."

She blushed. Way to go not thinking about sex for a whole twenty seconds.

He tapped the end of her nose and smiled. "While I would like nothing more than to discuss *that* particular position with you, let's wait until we meet your wolf."

Holy. God.

Okay, now she truly didn't know what was going on.

And frankly, right then, she didn't care.

"As I was saying," Parker continued. "When you're ready, you'll close your eyes and imagine the moon. She's already out, full and bright, ready to wash over you and bring your new inner wolf out into the open. There's a… bond for lack of a better word between you and your wolf. Find that small thread that will one day be something far stronger and tug on it. I know it sounds weird, but if you visualize what you will be, what you have become, it will be much easier."

His thumb traced along her jaw, and for some reason, with him near, she knew she could do this. She could find her new path...the path she'd seen in a vision she hadn't been meant to have. Was it because of the type of wolf he was, the Voice of the Wolves, the mediator? Or was it because he was Parker? She thought it could be the former, but perhaps it was the latter because Brandon did the same thing to her.

Once again, she wondered how on earth she'd ended up here, yet it didn't matter. She was here now, and worrying about things that couldn't be changed wasn't going to help her figure this out.

"I won't lie," Parker whispered, "this will hurt. All changing hurts, but your first time as an adult will hurt more than anything you've been through. As children, those born into our life are shielded from the pain by the moon goddess. We learn what the shift feels like *without* pain so we can find that thread and shift easier as adults—even with the pain. Those bitten do not have that luxury, and for that, I am sorry."

She met his gaze, his eyes gold. That meant his wolf was close to the surface according to what she'd read. Interesting. "I remember the attack," she said after a moment. "Not all, but I remember the first bite."

He cursed. "This might hurt more. There's nothing to be done, no drugs to help, no other wolf that can take away that pain. Maybe we're like the humans say and we're truly cursed."

She shook her head. "Those humans who say such things know nothing."

Parker's hand on her face tightened fractionally before dropping away. "You are truly a remarkable person, Avery."

She shook her head, pulling away from his touch, though she didn't want to leave the warmth of him. "No. I'm not." She tugged on the hem of her shirt. "Let's do this." Going fast so she wouldn't think too hard, she stripped down to the skin, ignoring Parker's gaze as he did the same. He didn't look below her face, though and she couldn't help but feel slightly better. Apparently, wolves were just fine with nudity, and she was going to have to get over her own insecurities—but she hadn't missed the heat in his eyes.

He wanted her.

One more thing to worry about. Later, however, because as the moon danced along her skin, she felt its pull.

And it *hurt*.

She lowered herself to the ground, the leaves and grass beneath her skin biting, but anchoring at the same time. She couldn't forget who she was, even if she was now something different.

"Find that thread and tug," Parker whispered by her side. He set his large palm on her back, and she stiffened before forcing herself to relax. It was just so *hard*—pun intended—since the man was seriously attractive and naked beside her.

But she wasn't going to look. This time.

For a woman who had visions of the future, kneeling in the grass naked next to an equally naked man and trying to turn into a wolf seemed *really* weird to her. But she was going to do it anyway because something deep inside told her that this was what she'd been destined to do all along—even if she hadn't understood.

She focused on the imaginary threads she figured surrounded the bright, white ball of light within her. Maybe that's not what a soul looked like, but it had been the first thing she'd thought of. As soon as she felt the fragile, thin thread that spoke of forest and yearning, she tugged, hoping she was doing this right.

Avery screamed out in pain, her bones shaking and her muscles on the verge of tearing.

"You're doing it, Avery. Keep going."

Apparently, she had been doing it right, but now that this pain kept cascading over her, she wasn't sure she wanted to keep going...only, she had to. There was no other way.

She tugged again, this time throwing her head back in a scream that somehow became a howl. Her tendons snapped, her bones elongating after breaking and reforming. Her muscles tore, and her body broke out in a sweat before fur sprouted.

Sweet agony, she thought. A sweet agony.

And then she was Avery, human, vision holder, and daughter of a traitor no more.

Now, she was all of those things and *wolf*.

"You're a gorgeous wolf," Parker said from her side. "You did brilliantly. Even faster than some of the teenagers we have, who have been shifting for a decade. I'm going to shift, as well, and then we can run. Let your wolf to the surface, not just in body, but also in mind. She won't lead you wrong, but you need to *run*."

It was weird, being one thing she'd never been before and yet having it feel so right. And when Parker stood before her as a tall, dark, and fierce wolf, she followed him, letting her wolf do what it needed to do. She tripped at first, then just *was*. They ran through the forest, her new Pack alongside her, her Alpha rubbing his head along hers and nipping at her neck to show she was his. Her heart thudded, and her senses were overwhelmed, but she was *free*.

And when she caught a familiar scent on the breeze, along with food and warmth, she followed it, Parker at her side. Brandon stood at the forest's edge, a plate of food in his hands, and their clothes in the other.

"Shift back a little early this time," Brandon explained, the dark shadows under his eyes intense. He hadn't been able to shift with them that night, and she needed to know why.

There was something wrong with both Brandon and Parker, and now that Avery had this...connection with them, she knew she had to help. But first, she had to become Avery again and not wolf.

The shift back to human was just as painful as going the other way, but this time, she wasn't as scared. With these two by her side, she knew they'd never again let harm come to her if they could help it. Why she felt so strongly about that, she didn't know, but she wasn't about to take it for granted.

Brandon silently held out her clothes, and she blushed, pulling them on quickly. She wasn't sure she'd ever get used to the whole nudity thing—even if the others didn't seem to care. Only she'd caught the same look in his eyes that Parker had given her earlier. Once again...interesting.

"I have some cold beef and pasta," Brandon explained, holding out the plate. "Not much, but enough to get you and Parker going until we get more food in you. The change takes more energy out of you than you think, so you need to replenish."

Parker reached out and grabbed one of the forks as well as the plate from Brandon. Brandon held the other fork out, a piece of beef on the end.

She did the only thing that came natural and bent forward to take a bite. She didn't miss the intensity of Brandon's gaze when she did that.

Brandon cleared his throat. "You're going to need to eat a lot more than you're used to from now on."

She tilted her head, taking another bite from him. Maybe this was the new wolf in her because she didn't think having him feed her was too weird, but still. She took the fork from him after the second bite and went to finish her half of the plate since Parker had already inhaled his. They were right that she'd be hungry, and she hadn't even known it.

"Are you eating enough then if Leah mentioned you only drink protein shakes?"

Parker gave Brandon a pointed look that she didn't understand. "Let's get back to the house. It's your first night there."

She frowned, not missing the fact that he'd sidestepped her question to Brandon but stood up. "What's going to happen to my place? I mean, my real home."

"It's not safe for you outside of the den right now, at least until we figure out who attacked you and why," Brandon said. "As for your place, we can have someone go and get your things if you want."

She held up her hands as they entered the house. She'd seen it once before, but she hadn't gotten a real good look. "As much as I appreciate everything you're doing, you need to stop making decisions for me. And don't tell me you know best. That might be the case, but I need options so *I* can make my own decisions."

"The Alpha might have something to say about that," Parker added dryly.

"Like he's taking care of the wolf that hurt me?"

Brandon's eyes darkened. "He's dealing with the Aspens." She knew of the Pack by name, but didn't know much about them.

She growled, surprising herself. She didn't growl, but then again, she was wolf now. Maybe growling was what she did.

"Maybe you should sit down," Parker said calmly, annoying her.

"I don't need to rest, and you know it," Avery bit out. "I just shifted into a freaking wolf for the first time, and now I'm about to stay under a roof with two men I don't know but for some reason feel a connection to. So, yeah, things are a little out of my control right now, and if it's all right with you, I'd like to make a decision on my own about my things. Is that okay? I don't know what is going on with that other Pack, but I know I'm going to need answers eventually. The only thing I *can* control right now is what happens to my possessions."

The vision hit her before they could respond, and she fell to her knees. Visions didn't always hit this hard, but when they did, she knew she had no hope of controlling them. Yet she knew *this* vision was going to be different. They had never slammed into her with this much intensity. She could practically taste the new air, feel the breeze on her cheek.

Being bitten by that wolf had done more to her than turn her into a shifter. Of that, she was sure.

In the vision, Parker and Brandon were wrapped around one another in the grass, fighting for control as their mouths met, their bodies thrusting against one another as if they couldn't wait to get their jeans off. They panted, their bodies becoming one, their wolves howling in pleasure.

Somehow, she found the strength to pull herself out of the vision, sweat breaking out over her body.

Ah. So it seemed the two men were for each other. Not for her. Okay, then. She'd just have to get over this attraction and deal with it—though the vision she'd just had was the sexiest thing she'd ever seen, and if she'd been alone, she might have done something to take care of the sudden need washing over her.

"Holy shit," Brandon gasped.

"You're a foreseer," Parker breathed.

She blinked, now aware that she knelt between the two of them, their hands keeping her upright. "What?" She blinked again before looking between them. "Did I... did I just say all of that aloud?"

She didn't do that often and had trained herself *not* to do it in fact, but with everything that had happened, her defenses must have been down.

Avery tried to pull away from the men but found she couldn't. Instead, the two of them let her go after making sure she wouldn't sway or fall again. She licked her lips, embarrassed at not only what she might have said, but the fact that her secret was truly out. If these two knew, then the rest of the Pack would know soon.

What would they do to her? Would they expect her to perform for them often? Like a trained monkey? Would they kill her outright for fear of what she would see? Would they tear her apart to see how she ticked...just like her father had done to her mother?

Her breath came in chopping pants, and both men put their hands on her arms, calming her. How did they keep doing that? It didn't make sense.

"Breathe," Parker whispered. "Just breathe."

"It was like you were reading subtitles," Brandon said after a moment, answering her question from before.

"You told us what you were seeing." Parker coughed. "Then, uh...said that you were going to take care of something yourself."

Well, apparently, she *had* said it all. If a hole in the floor could just open up now and bury her, that would be fantastic.

"So, I'm just going to blow right past all of that," she said after a moment. "For now. Yes, I have visions. If you call those who do foreseer, then yes, I'm a foreseer. I have been since I was a child, but they've never been this clear...this *intense* before." She was sure the heat radiating off her face could have warmed the entire planet. She'd just confessed to seeing these two men going at it and then said she wanted to get herself off watching them. Seriously, she needed that hole to open up any minute now.

"You're connected to the moon goddess," Brandon said softly. "Maybe that intensified your visions."

She put a hand over her stomach, nausea welling. "I don't know if I like that."

He gave her a look of pity that she didn't like. "I know what you mean." Oh, right, he was the Omega. He didn't have control over everything warring in him thanks to the moon goddess either.

"You also said you weren't for us," Parker said with a

frown. "That once you saw Brandon and me together, that you were going to step away." He tilted his head. "I don't know...I..."

Brandon cursed. "The mating bonds are different now," he bit out, and Parker's head shot to the other man.

"What?"

"I can't explain it, but ever since Shane came into the Pack with whatever Montag put into his system, something has been off with the mating bonds. Things our wolves should be saying or doing aren't happening like they used to."

"I don't understand," Avery cut in. "What did my dad do?"

Brandon cursed. "I'm sorry. I keep forgetting he's your father."

"Glad one of us can," she murmured.

Parker squeezed her hand. "Your dad made a serum that he thought would create wolves. It didn't work."

Shock and anger tore through Avery. "I...I'm so sorry."

They waved her off, and Parker continued. "The way matings are supposed to work is that our wolves tell us when there is a potential mate near. The mating urge riles us up, and we *need* to bond, though we do have choices."

"That's how it used to be," Brandon whispered. "But I don't think that's the way things are anymore. I think...I think the human part needs to sense something first, and then the wolf will come about. I don't know *how* I know that, but I do. And that means the way our wolves find our mates has forever changed."

"Holy shit," Parker breathed.

Avery shook her head, her brain not quite catching up to everything. "Explain. You can't say you just *know* things. I get that you're all supernatural and things come from your goddess, but I need more facts than you just...know."

Brandon let out a sigh and sank down onto the couch. She and Parker followed, each keeping just enough distance that she knew they'd done it on purpose. "My wolf is closer to the base instincts than others. I can tell what anyone is feeling at any given moment as long as their shields aren't locked down tight. Anyone in my Pack, that is," he added quickly. "There have been a few instances where I've watched wolves come close to one another, find that attraction, but not find the bond. They're left confused, and it rushes through me like a wave. Now, with the two of you? I don't know what's going on, but I *know* something is off. Something that should have been shown to us right away but is apparently hiding...or maybe even broken."

Avery gripped the edge of the couch, confused as ever. "That doesn't mean..." She paused, trying to collect her thoughts. "So that might mean that you and Parker are mates. I *saw* it in that vision. Maybe there is something off with mating bonds, but I don't have anything to do with it."

Parker leaned forward, cupping Avery's face. She froze, scared that he might do something that could change *everything*.

"You might have everything to do with it."

Then he kissed her.

CHAPTER 7

AVERY REMAINED stiff under Parker's touch for a bare moment before she let out a soft moan. Parker was aware that Brandon was right next to him, breathing heavily as he watched.

Parker had been thinking about kissing Avery from the moment he first saw her, even if he had been on edge, wondering if she were a danger to the Pack. She tasted of sweetness and wolf, the perfect combination that he hadn't known he craved.

He licked her bottom lip as he pulled away, aware more needed to be said before he gave in to his wolf...and himself.

Avery let out a breath. "Why did you do that?"

"Because I needed to," he answered honestly. "I don't

know what's going on, but there's something…there's something between the three of us." He looked over at Brandon, who stared at him and Avery with a curious expression on his face. "Can you feel it?"

It wasn't his wolf pushing at him, wanting her as his mate, wanting Brandon as his mate. It was something far different. But if what Brandon said was true, then none of the wolves were going to find their other halves the way they had for centuries.

The ramifications were staggering.

She tilted her head, confusion written all over her face. "I feel…something. But I don't understand what's going on."

"What's going on is that Parker and I have done our best to stay away from one another as much as we could because we thought we weren't mates," Brandon bit out. "We both need to find our mate—or mates—soon because…well, his secret is not mine to tell, and tonight is a little heavy to go into all of my secrets. But in the end, I've done everything I could to make sure I didn't make a mistake, that I didn't fall for someone that could end up watching me fade away because I wasn't the right wolf for them. And in the end, it seems none of that mattered. There's something wrong with the way our bonds are forming, the way our wolves can recognize each other. I don't know how we're going to fix that or if there's an answer to what we need at all, but what I do know is that you had a vision of Parker and me, and I can tell you that Parker isn't the only one who wants you."

Avery's eyes widened, and Parker took a deep breath, knowing this was all way too much for anyone all at once.

"How about we take a break?" Parker said softly. "Get some food, talk about the run, then come back to this another night. Whatever *this* is. I feel like we're talking in circles because we're exhausted and not thinking straight. And with what's to come—not with just us, but with our Packs and the world—I feel like we need our wits about us."

He cupped Avery's face with one hand, taking Brandon's hand with the other. "Let's just be…just for the moment. Then we'll figure out what's going on."

"Ever the mediator," Brandon murmured.

"I have no idea what I got myself into," Avery added.

"Neither do we," Parker agreed. "But I think we might get more than we ever bargained for in the best possible way."

At least, he hoped so. Because if Brandon and Avery were indeed his mates…then that meant he would live. He would be able to take another breath, knowing that he could find the strength to protect those he loved. And through it all…he'd find his happiness.

He just prayed that this wasn't all a lie.

Because if that were the case…then he'd not only have no more time to find his true mate, but he'd end up hurting two people he was starting to care about more than he thought possible.

REVOLT

McMaster watched the footage for the sixth time, a manic energy riding him as a small smile threatened to appear. He couldn't let the others see him smile at this, couldn't let a single person know his true desires. He might be alone in the room while he watched the woman be attacked by a wolf, but someone could walk in at any moment.

He lived in DC, after all, and no place was truly private. Not anymore.

When McMaster let the wolf 'escape' from captivity after the year of study he had arranged, he'd known something like this would happen—only not on this scale.

He'd known humans would be near the den since there were groups of them roaming around the area often

—either those perpetuating the anti-wolf movement or clusters of the tree-hugging, wolf-lover types. He'd just needed one of them to get a little too close to *his* wolf for his plan to work.

The fact that it had been his former accomplice's daughter in the line of fire had made it that much juicer. He'd known of the woman's existence, of course, even if Montag had done his best to cut all ties with her—emotionally and physically. McMaster didn't work with just *anyone* to end up where he was in his life.

And when the world saw that it was Montag's daughter, they would see it as retaliation, not an accident. They would see the shifters attacking a defenseless woman because of who her father had been. Montag had killed shifters, so they had murdered what was left of his line.

McMaster was a U.S. Senator, leader of the Wolf Inhuman Campaign, and future President of the United States if this next election cycle were anything to go by. People loved him, they revered him, and they trusted him to get rid of that pesky wolf problem.

And for those who might want the wolves to stay alive? Well, that was why he'd soon be sharing the images of Avery's attack. A vicious wolf killing a harmless woman just on a walk through the woods. What kind of monster would allow these...beasts the ability to breathe?

His people had ensured that all video surveillance of the Talon area where he'd let his rogue wolf roam was strictly under his command. Meaning the world hadn't yet seen the true natures of these creatures, the depravity that came with being an *animal*.

And in twenty minutes, he'd step out onto the stage and show his fellow Americans how truly horrific these wolves were. This woman had *died* because of the gross negligence of these wolves' supposed leaders.

He'd ask how they could let their children out in the world, knowing these monsters could bite and tear their flesh before they'd even made it to the school bus.

The shifter advocacy groups spoke of the fear that came from not understanding, well, McMaster would twist that to his advantage. He would make sure that everyone understood exactly what he wanted them to. The media loved him and gave him the airtime he needed to ensure that every single person in America knew his face and his message.

The wolves needed to be eradicated from the world, and McMaster would be there to ensure that happened. And when the country saw him as their savior, they would vote him into office.

And everything he'd worked for, everything he'd made others bleed for, would finally come to fruition.

McMaster stood, straightening his tie. It was time the world saw the shifters for who and what they were. And the bloodless body of Montag's daughter would be the face of the movement.

Revolution had never come so easily.

CHAPTER 8

"WHAT WE'RE SEEING HERE IS nothing short of murder," McMaster said in a crisp voice as Brandon watched from his living room. "These shifters are not human. They are not like us. They need to be controlled so our children and everything we've fought for can be preserved. Without order, without control, these shifters will kill anyone who stands in their way of power. As you can see from this video surveillance, they attacked a lone woman walking in the forest alone. She had done nothing wrong except be the daughter of a man they hate. They ignored law, ignored policy, and took revenge into their own hands. How can this be allowed in our society? If we forsake what we know, forsake our laws and morals, would we not become the animals that hunt us like this poor woman?"

Knees shaky, Brandon sank down onto the couch, Avery by his side. Parker sat on the other edge of the couch, and all three of them focused on the horror unfolding in front of them.

"They think I'm dead," Avery said after a moment. "They think a Talon member killed me for revenge." Her body tensed next to him, and Brandon put his hand on her shoulder, taking in some of her pain. He shuddered, the intensity of her anguish a mark on his soul, but he kept going. "Stop it, Brandon," she whispered. "You're hurting yourself, and I need this anger."

Brandon shook his head. "You don't need all of it. No one can think clearly with all of that bottled up inside of them."

Avery glared at him but didn't say anything. His wolf wanted to help her more, but he held back, knowing if he did too much, too soon, he'd break the fragile trust she'd placed in him.

"At times like these, I wish I were a Talon," Parker said after a moment, and Brandon turned to the other man.

"What?" he asked.

"You two have a connection I don't have. I'm a strange wolf in a different den. Sometimes, I miss my Pack." He shrugged, and Brandon knew there was more than what Parker was saying. "As for what McMaster is saying…"

"Not everyone is going to believe him, right?" Avery asked, desperation in her voice. "What if I told them I was alive?"

Brandon shook his head. "Then you tell the world you are wolf. Is that something you're ready for? Because you'll be the true evidence of how shifters are made. They might think they know, but the world doesn't know the truth behind it all."

"And people are afraid, Avery," Parker added, bringing Brandon's attention to him. "They're so afraid of what could happen, that they'll listen to anyone with a platform and a plan—no matter how vague or damaging it is."

"It wasn't you, though," she growled before standing up to pace in front of the screen. Brandon had muted the television right after the senator's speech so they wouldn't have to listen to the unending dissection of the man's damaging words by the media.

Brandon could sense her wolf rising, and he stood up with her so he could make sure she didn't do anything that could hurt her. She'd only been a shifter for a few days, and there was no way she could be expected to have the kind of control she needed during a true bout of anger. That was one reason he'd siphoned off some of her rage earlier, though he hadn't mentioned that—although he should because she honestly needed all the facts.

"Avery," he said slowly, the tone of the Omega in his voice. "You need to calm down or your wolf will come out and you might end up hurting yourself."

"He's right," Parker put in. "You're not ready to do a partial shift, and I don't even think you could if you tried at this point. So, if you let your wolf get too close to the surface, you'll either shift fully when you're not ready, or pass out from the pain."

Avery put her hands on her hips and glared at the two of them. "So I can't feel what I need to feel now? Is that the case?"

Brandon reached out and cupped her face. "I know you didn't ask for this, but you live with another soul deep inside you now. You have another part of you that is vying for control, even if it doesn't know how to do that yet. You're going to have to control your emotions and reactions even if it doesn't seem fair. Parker and I aren't telling you to let this go, and we're damn well not telling you to ignore what you're feeling, but we want you to be aware of it."

"He's right, Avery," Parker said softly from beside Brandon. The three of them were standing close enough that he could feel their combined heat. And if he weren't careful, Brandon would be the one ignoring reason and listening to his base instincts. "We're going to fight this. We've been fighting for our people since before the

Unveiling and we're not going to stop now. You're one of us, and that means you're under our protection."

Her eyes glowed gold, and Brandon's wolf perked up—exhausted as it was. He had a feeling once she settled into her new role, she'd be a dominant—perhaps even as dominant as he and Parker. It excited him to no end, but he put that aside, knowing it wasn't the time. "I need to learn to protect myself," she bit out. "I've been doing that for my entire life and I'm not going to suddenly want to rely on other people because they say it'll be easier. I came to the den to help, and now I'm suddenly a shifter and locked away in a house."

Brandon stepped forward and cupped her face. Her cheeks heated under his palms, and he did his best to keep his libido under control. "We're not your jailers. You have free rein of the den, though I think one of us should be with you for the time being while the others get used to you. Our Pack wasn't always as healthy as it is now, and while you should be safe, there are those who might see you as the reason they fear."

Parker cursed at his words and moved so they stood side-to-side. The other man wrapped his arms around Avery's hips, bringing the three of them closer than they had ever been before.

From the way his dick responded, Brandon liked it far more than he should.

"What he's trying to say is that no den is perfect, and you're not in jail. You're still new, so wolves might feel the need to see who is more dominant. Those challenges happen often to new wolves or those who gain in power when their wolf is ready. It's not just you. Believe me. And as much as I'd love for you to feel free to leave the den, right now, it's not a good idea. No one in the Pack is safe out there, and I don't think we will be until this whole thing comes to an end."

Avery studied them both before pulling away slightly. The movement ended with all three of them tangled a bit—a touch here, a caress there—but they still stood in their makeshift circle in the end. "I just hate feeling out of control. I will forever be grateful that you saved me and opened your home to me, but I might still feel a little resentful for the way things worked out, as well."

Brandon nodded. "We're complex like humans in that respect—we're allowed to feel more than one thing at a time."

"Shocking, I know."

Avery let out a shaky breath. "Holy shit, I'm not human anymore."

"It'll take time to get used to," Brandon responded. "And now you have more time than before for that to happen."

Her eyes widened and she leaned into Parker a

moment before seeming to realize what she'd done and straightening herself. "Well, hell. I just...it's a lot to take in, you know? I mean, it should be easier for me since I've been able to see the future and knew I was going to one day be a wolf, but still."

All three of them froze at her words.

"You knew?" Brandon rasped.

She swallowed hard, fear radiating off her. "Yes, but only in a blurred way. I didn't know how or why or when. Just that one day, I would run on four paws. I've never seen myself in a vision before other than that, so I didn't understand what it meant."

"We're going to have to tell Gideon everything," Parker said. "Kade, as well. We should have already, but we were giving you time."

She nodded. "I understand. I'm sorry that I kept things from everyone in the first place."

Brandon studied her face. "We all have our secrets."

She tilted her head. "And what secrets are those? Because if you're saying I might be your mate, I'd like to know them." She bit her lip. "I mean, if that's still an option or something or...you know, I'll stop rambling now."

Brandon traced his finger along her jaw, taking in the way she shivered at his touch but didn't back away. He didn't know if what they wanted would be the right thing, but then again, nothing worth having was ever easy. Yes, he and Parker each needed their mates to survive—though the other man had yet to explain why—but risking their hearts and bodies for a bond that might never come could hurt them more in the end.

"We're in uncharted territory here." Brandon put a hand on Parker's side so the three were fully connected once again. "I don't know what the right answer is, other than I *know* there is something between us."

Parker narrowed his eyes. "And you also know that if you don't get a mate soon, you'll die. Isn't that right?"

Avery backed away, eyes wide. "What does he mean by that, Brandon?"

Brandon lifted his chin, knowing that his secrets weren't so secret anymore, at least under this roof. "As the Omega, I'm connected to each and every Pack member. It takes…a toll on me every time I need to use my senses to comfort or soothe high-strung emotions."

Avery pushed at his chest. "And yet you keep trying to make sure I feel better? Why would you do that? You need to let me be and let me learn to control this new wolf inside of me. I won't be responsible for hurting you." Tears filled her eyes, and she angrily blinked them back. "I've only spent a few days with you and Parker, but in that time, I feel like I've gotten to know you more and more. I don't want to hurt the man I've learned to like…learned that my wolf—if that's what I'm truly feeling—wants to know more. You guys saved my life but you also let me *be*. You listened to me when I was afraid that no one else would. There's something between us, I can feel it, too, but I don't want you to hurt yourself because you have this self-destructing need to protect me." She looked at Parker. "I don't want *either* of you to hurt yourselves doing that."

Brandon narrowed his eyes at her, his own wolf perking up at the tone of her voice. She wanted them, *craved* them, and yet they were all holding back because they were so damned afraid of hurting one another.

"I can't help but be what I am, Avery. I'm the Omega. I'll *always* want to ensure those around me—those I care about—are taken care of. That's not something I can control any more than you can control your temper at the moment. We're not human."

"He's right," Parker said. "We're not human. That means whatever we feel sometimes is a hundred-times stronger than what we would have felt if we hadn't been born wolves. When we want someone, we take him or her because usually, the other person wants us just as much. We give in to our urges at times because not doing so would only make it worse."

Avery licked her lips, her gaze shooting between him

and Parker, and Brandon did his best not to think about her tongue on his cock.

"You didn't finish what you were saying earlier," Avery said after a moment. "What does that mean, about you being the Omega? Why do you need a mate?"

"Because being the Omega means you give more of yourself," Parker answered for him, and for that, Brandon was grateful. It wasn't always easy to talk about what he did day in and day out, but Parker seemed to understand. The man had a way of knowing exactly what a person needed without asking, and Brandon had a feeling it wasn't because of any special powers. Parker was just that kind of man.

"And?" Avery's voice had gone soft.

"And if he doesn't find someone to share the burden, he might give more of himself than he has to give."

"That's not the only reason I want a mate," Brandon countered. "It's part of it, but I also want a mate because I'm over a hundred years old and would like to share my life with someone." *Or someones.*

Avery moved forward, placing her hand on his chest. "I'm a...foreseer. I know what it's like to not be able to control part of yourself. I feel like my body's out of my control, and I have to give in to what the powers that be need me to see. So I get it." She paused. "I really do."

Brandon looked down at her, his body stiff. Maybe she

did understand, and that scared him. He hated that sometimes he couldn't control the wave of pain and dizziness that came with his duty to his people or what happened when he passed out thanks to a flare in the wards. Yet this woman—this female who had only just become wolf—seemed to understand.

Pairing that with the fact that he *knew* something similar was happening to Parker, and Brandon felt a wave of peace wash over him for the first time in months.

He looked up at Parker and cursed. "You're pale. Too pale."

Parker coughed. "I'm fine." Then his knees gave out. Brandon moved past Avery in an instant and caught the other man before he fell completely. Avery was right behind him and helped to get Parker sitting on the couch.

"Okay, so we know what's going on with Brandon," Avery said quickly, her voice on the edge of panic. "Now why don't you tell me what's going on with you."

Parker wiped away the sweat from his face with his forearm. "I don't know completely. Only that, like Brandon, I need a mate, too."

Brandon cursed. "Tell us what you *do* know."

Parker swallowed hard, and Brandon sank to his knees by the other man's legs while Avery knelt between them, her body shaking. Brandon put his hand on the small of her back and she settled somewhat. He hoped to the goddess he never got over that thrill of seeing her calm under his touch.

"I was in one of the European Packs' den, and caught a disease that only runs in my line, apparently. They said if I don't find a mate, it'll slowly eat away at me."

Brandon let out a breath slowly. "Your *line*? As in the first hunter's line?" The Talons knew the story of Parker's ancestry that came from his mother. The family had originally been Talons, after all.

"The first hunter?" Avery asked.

"My ancestor was the hunter who the moon goddess cursed, for lack of a better word, to become the prey he'd killed. He was the first shifter."

"And the Talons were the first Pack," Brandon added.

Avery sank down so her butt rested on her feet and leaned into Brandon. "So let me get this straight. You both need mates to survive, yet the way shifters have been trying to find mates all this time has completely changed thanks to a human-made serum that was supposed to make shifters but failed horribly?"

Leave it to Avery to put something like that into one sentence.

Parker snorted and winced. Brandon ran his hand down the other man's arm before tangling his fingers with his. The other man wasn't Pack, so that meant he couldn't find a way to Heal him, but he could at least be there for him. What Parker had said also explained why he wasn't staying with the Redwoods. The last of Parker's line still lived there, and Brandon guessed that no one knew how contagious he might be.

"Pretty much," Parker said, his color coming back. "The waves of pain come and go so I can usually hide it pretty well. Though it's hard to do when I'm living with another person. But I usually bounce back right away, and in a few minutes, I'll feel perfectly fine."

"Only you *aren't* perfectly fine," Avery countered. "Neither of you are. And now that you can't sense who your mate will be, you don't know what the next step is."

"We'll find a way," Brandon said softly. "We have to."

"How? By hoping the old ways come back?" Avery shook her head. "Or maybe you should see what happens when you take the first step you would in a normal mating and see if something changes."

Brandon blinked. "Do you know the steps of mating?"

Avery blushed. "Uh, no, but I figured it has to do with sex, right?"

Parker laughed, and thankfully, didn't cough afterward. The man looked exactly like he had before he'd gotten sick a few moments ago, and that worried Brandon. If he could so easily hide what was going on with him, what else was Brandon missing?

"Sex, yes," Parker said. "There are two parts of the

mating. Sex to create the bond between the humans. A biting mark to create the bond between our wolves. For those who don't know if they're ready to complete the mating fully but still want each other, they forgo the mating mark until the mating urge is riding them too hard for them to hold back any longer. Either that, or they walk away, knowing they might lose part of themselves in the process."

"The moon goddess is never wrong," Brandon added. "But she also gives us the option."

"And now you can't hear what she wants," Avery said. "Because of what the serum did."

Brandon nodded. "When we added Shane to the Pack, we twisted the way our Pack works. Or at least the ways the bonds work. It's not like when there were demons added to the Packs—those were already paranormal."

"Demons?" Avery squeaked.

"Long story," Parker said quickly. "Long story I'd rather not get into tonight."

"This whole paranormal world is far bigger than what the rest of the world knows, isn't it?"

"Far bigger," Brandon agreed. "But we keep things secret for a reason. You yourself have a touch of something that another human might not understand. I take it that's why you're not running screaming from the room when we're talking about mates and bonds."

"It would be hypocritical of me to do so. And now that I literally just ran on four legs as a wolf, I really can't hide from what's out there." She took a deep breath. "So I'm not going to hide from this. The three of us feel something. Maybe it's just attraction, and I can understand that. Hell, you're both so freaking sexy it's really hard to pay attention when you're in the room. And I've seen the way you each look at me so I know you at least find me somewhat attractive."

"That's an understatement," Parker mumbled under his breath, and Brandon held back a laugh. It was good to see the wolf back to his normal self again.

"So why don't we try out the first part of the mating to see if it sticks. I mean, I'm *so* not ready to create a full mating bond because I need to not only get to know you first, but I'd like to get to know who I am now, as well. But we can see if we're mates this way. Or, at least try."

Brandon blinked, at a loss for words.

"Are you saying you want to have sex with us to see if we're all mates?" Parker asked slowly.

"Yes. I mean, it's literally life or death." Avery's eyes were wide, and if it weren't for the fact that he could hear her heart beating frantically, he'd have thought this was a normal conversation for her.

Nothing in his Pack these days was normal it seemed. Brandon couldn't help himself, he laughed.

"What?" Avery asked, laughter dancing in her eyes, as well.

"The absurdity of this conversation," Brandon said after he could catch his breath. "You're saying we should have sex to save our lives."

"Sounds a little B-rated movie to me," Parker added, deadpan.

Avery threw up her hands and stood up. "Okay, fine. It does sound a little weird, but come on. All three of us want each other. I *know* it, so you'd better not deny it."

Brandon shook his head. "I won't deny it."

"No denial here either."

"Then what's the problem?" Avery asked.

"What if we're not mates?" Brandon said softly, voicing his true fear.

Avery pressed her lips together before letting out a breath. "Then we aren't, but we'll be good friends who had one night of amazing sex. Because it will be amazing. And with the tension in this room and outside the house, I think a little sex might be exactly what we need."

"And what if we *are* mates?" Parker asked. "What then?"

Avery twisted her hands together. "Then we deal with that when the time comes. But if we walk away because we're too scared to do anything about it, then we'll regret it for the rest of our lives."

Parker met Brandon's gaze. "What are your thoughts?"

He hadn't known what he would say until the words tumbled from his mouth. "I want you. I've always wanted you. Why do you think I fight with you so much?" He turned to Avery. "And I want you, too, but are you sure you can deal with *both* of us? Triads aren't uncommon in our world, but I know for a fact that humans don't usually know how to deal with them."

Avery raised her chin. "I think the better question, boys, is if *you* can handle *me*."

Brandon was on his feet before his next breath, his mouth crushing down on Avery's as she opened her mouth in surprise. She leaned into him, her hands running down his sides as he cupped her face, angling her head so he could deepen the kiss.

His wolf pawed at him, needing to be closer. They both knew that this could just be for heat, just for need, and that the bond might never show up, but at that moment, with this woman in his arms and Parker so close, he didn't care. He just wanted them. *Needed* them.

Somehow, the three of them were standing together, Brandon's arms around Avery as he kissed her, Parker's hands trailing up both of their backs at the same time.

Then Brandon pulled away, and Parker had his lips on Avery, their moans making Brandon's already hard cock harder. Brandon licked up Avery's neck, biting down softly.

The other man pulled away from Avery and kissed Brandon, rough but soft at the same time. Brandon loved both of their tastes separately, but when they were together...Brandon thought he might pass out from it all.

Parker had his hand down Brandon's pants in the next blink, and Brandon almost lost it right there. He pulled away, panting as he reached forward to slide his hand up Avery's shirt. As soon as he cupped her breast, the three of them groaned, their bodies moving faster. Somehow, everyone had a hand on each other, cocks being stroked, Avery's wet heat around Brandon's fingers, then Parker. Between panting, they each stripped to the skin, bodies thrumming. He was so lost in the haze of sex and need that Brandon almost tripped over a pair of pants. He cursed.

"Fuck it. We need the bedroom."

Parker grinned. "Sounds like a plan. I want to lick Avery up until she comes on both of our faces and it's kind of hard to do that in the living room."

Before Avery had a chance to say anything to that, Brandon kissed her hard again, this time picking her up by palming her ass and carrying her to his bedroom. Since he had the master, he also had the larger bed—though he was afraid a king might not even be big enough for the three of them.

Brandon kissed Avery again before laying her down on the mattress, her legs spread before them.

"You know, I never actually thought about the logistics of how this would work," Avery said, her face flushed.

"Liar," Parker said with a grin as he knelt beside Brandon between Avery's legs. "You've thought about *exactly* how this is going to work."

Brandon hadn't thought it was possible, but Avery turned even redder.

"Okay, fine, I thought about having sex with both of you and even at the same time, but I didn't actually think about the positions beyond fuzzy ideas. I've never actually been in a threesome before."

Brandon looked at Parker, who shook his head. "I guess we'll just go with what feels right." He cleared his throat. "But in order for the mating to possibly show itself…"

Parker leaned forward and kissed him gently, his eyes dark with lust. "You'll have to take me, as well. I know." He turned to Avery. "We'll all get a turn, darling, but since he's the one who *can't* leave his Pack, he's the one who gets to fuck me first."

Avery's mouth parted, and she licked her lips. "Not

gonna lie, I want to see *both* of you take each other. If that's what you want."

Parker looked at Brandon and smiled. "I'm game with either."

Brandon kissed the man who could be his mate again, sliding his hand between them to grip Parker's cock. Then he thrust his inside his fist, as well and slid the two lengths against each other. Parker groaned, and Avery sat up to lean on her arms, her gaze transfixed on Brandon's hand.

"I'm game with whatever lets me touch the two of you," Brandon finally said.

"Good." Then Parker kissed him again before leaning between Avery's legs to lick at her. Avery's head fell back, and Brandon leaned forward, as well, licking and biting up her inner thigh. Together, he and Parker sucked at her, biting gently before kissing and licking her clit and lower lips. Their tongues tangled, and soon they were kissing each other at the same time they were making her come.

She reached for them, her body shaking as she came on their faces. "Oh my God. That was the sexiest thing I've ever seen in my life."

"And we're not even close to being done," Parker said with a grin. "Now, I'm thinking I want your mouth on my cock as Brandon enters you for the first time. Does that sound like a plan?"

Avery shivered, and Brandon squeezed the base of his

dick so he wouldn't come from Parker's words alone. The man could dirty talk like no other. When Brandon moved forward, Avery went to her hands and knees and smiled over her shoulder.

"Will this way work?" she asked, a wicked gleam in her eyes.

Brandon stepped forward and ran his hand down her hip and over the luscious curve of her ass. "Always."

She laughed then let out a groan when Parker went to kneel on the bed next to her face, his length hard and ready. She licked her lips before taking him into her mouth, and Brandon groaned before sliding deep into Avery's heat, inch by slow inch. As soon as he was fully seated, the three of them groaned, their bodies shaking.

"More," Avery panted before licking up Parker again.

Brandon knew he'd never felt as close to the heavens as he did just then and began to thrust in and out of her. Her body shook underneath him, and he knew she was close. Parker had bent forward to play with her breasts as she sucked him off, so Brandon bent over Avery's back to kiss him hard before going back to take a firm grip of her hips. He thrust harder, knowing they both needed more heat so they could fall over that edge together.

Then she came around him, her body tightening. And when he followed her, filling her with his seed, he felt the first snap of the bond take place. His wolf howled, his fangs elongated with the need to mark her, but he forced them back, knowing this wasn't the time.

But what he *did* know was that this woman, this amazingly smart and beautiful woman was his mate. That was why they hadn't used a condom, and why the thought hadn't even come up. They were wolves who didn't carry disease and could only get pregnant under full moons in the middle of a mating heat—or at least that's how the latter had always been. With so many things changing, that could, as well.

When Parker cupped his face, Brandon pushed away those thoughts and kissed the man back, his body ready to go again. He pulled away and slid out of Avery so she could roll onto her back, then bent over to press soft kisses over her stomach, her breasts, and to place a gentle kiss on her lips.

"I *feel* you," she said softly, her voice full of awe.

Brandon kissed her again. "You're everything, Avery. Never forget that. Now, are you ready for Parker to join us? That way, we can feel him, too?"

She slid her hand over his shoulder. "Of course, I'm ready. We need him, too."

Brandon straightened and moved back as Parker slid between them, a bottle of lube in his hand. He winked at him, and Brandon knew this wolf would forever make him smile if the fates let him.

"I'm going to make sure Avery is ready for me as well since it's going to be a long night," Parker said, and Avery let out a laugh.

"I'm pretty sure I've never been wetter, but go ahead and check." Her laugh cut off as Parker speared her with two fingers, and once again, Brandon had to grip himself so he wouldn't come. These two were going to be the death of him.

"Give me that," he bit out, his wolf on edge. He took the lube from Parker and kissed the other man's shoulder. "I don't want to hurt you."

Parker winked again. "I like a little bit of pain, but yeah, not *that* much."

Brandon let out a breath, trying to calm himself. "So have you bottomed before?"

Parker nodded. "I've always been bisexual, Brandon. And I like both topping and being a bottom."

Relief spread through Brandon. He didn't want to hurt Parker even if it was a good hurt. "Same here," he said after a moment. "Though it's been a while."

Avery sat up and ran her hand over Brandon's side. "Don't worry, baby, we'll be gentle."

Brandon snapped his teeth at her, and she jumped before the three of them let out a laugh. "Still a wolf, baby, I don't want gentle."

Avery's eyes went gold. "Good."

Then they touched, and kissed, their bodies moving as one as Parker slid into Avery, their moans turning Brandon on even more. Brandon made sure Parker was ready, gently probing him and ensuring that no matter what, he wouldn't hurt this man. Fangs and claws might be okay in the bedroom, but he didn't want to hurt him any other way.

As soon as Brandon pressed the tip of his erection to Parker's hole, the three of them froze.

"You ready?" Brandon asked, his voice a growl.

"Fuck me, Brandon," Parker bit out, his hands on Avery's hips. Their mate had wrapped her legs around both of them, though Brandon knew as soon as he fully entered Parker, she'd be able to hold on tighter.

"Anything you want." Then Brandon moved, and the three of them gasped. Every time Brandon thrust forward, it sent Parker deeper into Avery. With this position, the three of them ended up moving at a fluid rhythm, their bodies sweaty, heated, and on the edge of bliss once more.

Once again, Brandon's fangs elongated, the urge to mark and mate burning inside him. Brandon pushed the need back before he came at the same time as Parker. The two of them sent Avery over the edge once again, and the bond between the three of them shimmered for a moment, as if it were the symbol of what *could* be rather than what was.

They were potential mates—something that should have been apparent from the beginning but had been hidden from them. And with their joining, they'd started the first step of their mating. Without the mating mark, the connection between them would pulse for a while before fading away and forming into an intense mating urge.

They could either eventually give in or learn to ignore the need to mark each other and complete the mating.

Either way, Brandon knew this night had changed things.

He had his mates. His future in his hands.

Now, he just needed to figure out what to do about it.

CHAPTER 9

THE ACHES and pains running through Avery's body had nothing to do with the fact that she'd run as a wolf the night before. She blushed at the thought of what she, Parker, and Brandon had done, and knew she wanted to do it again.

She'd always been choosy in her bedmates, keeping her heart and her body guarded against those who could hurt her. Yet the two men who had made her come so many times the night before she'd lost count were different. Before she'd gone to bed with them, she thought she might be on the verge of losing her mind, but now, she knew that wasn't exactly true.

Brandon and Parker were her potential mates, and once they made the mating mark, they would be mates in truth.

The idea excited and overwhelmed her all at the same time.

The fact that she could still scent them on her skin was a whole other matter entirely.

If someone had asked her if she'd one day see herself writhing between two sweaty, delicious men and then below them both as they took each other, she'd have called them crazy. For a woman who saw the future, she surely hadn't seen this.

But now that they knew they could be mates, they had decisions to make. It wasn't inevitable that they'd end up together for eternity, and she was grateful for that. She needed time to think so she could wrap her head around the fact that she was not only a wolf in a time of war, but perhaps the mate of not one, but *two* dominant wolves.

Avery knew she didn't have much time to make decisions as both Parker and Brandon needed a mating bond quickly, but she was still grateful for what little time she had. This was all going a bit too fast for her, and while she'd been the one to initially suggest what had happened the night before, she still needed time to process it all.

While Parker was in the shower and Brandon in his bedroom on a conference call, Avery sat cross-legged in the living room, trying to center herself.

Okay, what had happened since she'd first had the

vision right before she'd seen the attack by her father on the Talons?

She'd come to the Talons with a small plan to try and help their image and have them using their own words for the masses. The Alphas still had not decided on that, and she had a feeling they were shelving it for the time being thanks to everything that had happened since their meeting. Avery wasn't even sure she'd have the same connections to the media as before thanks to the assault.

A rogue Aspen wolf had *attacked* her and, apparently, the Aspens weren't talking to the Talons about it. Avery didn't know much—or anything really—about wolf politics, but she had a feeling the lack of communication wasn't a good thing.

Because of the attack, Gideon had brought her into the Talon Pack, and she was now a wolf shifter. She'd had her first run, and Parker had helped her through her first change.

She was Pack now. Wolf. And falling for two men who had brought her to ecstasy countless times the night before.

What she would do with all of that, she didn't know, but she needed to think quickly. She had a feeling this tension-filled peace within the den would end soon. The ramifications of McMaster's plan would show their face any moment, and Avery was now the poster child for that plague.

Sweat broke out over her body, and she cursed. So much for trying to remain calm.

"Gideon wants to meet with us," Brandon said as he strode into the room. He stood right in front of her, a small smile on his face, though his eyes held the same danger she'd seen in them since she first met him.

Avery had scented Brandon before she saw him, and wasn't that a new and weird thing in her life. She had all these extra-sensitive senses now, and she had no idea what to do with them. If she didn't have Parker and Brandon showing her the ropes, she knew she'd be even more overwhelmed than she was. As it was, however, she knew she needed to take a step back and think. And she couldn't do that with the two men hovering over her as they were.

Avery rolled her shoulders as she took Brandon's outstretched hand and stood up, rubbing her body along his as she did. He let out a small growl, and she couldn't help the smile that played on her lips even as she blushed.

There was just something about this man—and the other man who'd just walked into the room—that made her want to stretch and lounge about like a cat in cream. Only she was a wolf, and there were far more important things to worry about at the moment.

"Did he say why?" Parker asked before placing a kiss

on her lips. He did the same to Brandon, and she let out a soft sigh.

These two men were going kill her with that hotness—but what a way to die.

"There's someone here to meet with you," Brandon said, a frown on his face. "He didn't say who, and was a little mysterious about it. Either way, he wants us all there since I think he wants to check in on Avery's well-being also."

"Because I shifted into a wolf last night, right? Not because he knows what happened between the three of us?"

Brandon shrugged. "My brother's the Alpha. He knows some things before the rest of us do."

"I thought I was the foreseer," she said dryly, even as her heart rate sped up.

Brandon dropped a kiss on her lips. "Let's go, if you're ready."

"As ready as I'll ever be."

Brandon squeezed her hand before heading to the front door. Parker slid behind her, one hand on the small of her back. It seemed the two were going to walk in this formation as if to protect her no matter what. And considering she wasn't sure how to fight and didn't know what would happen, she'd let them do this. For now.

When they made their way to the front gates, Gideon

stood there with his large arms crossed over his chest. When she'd been human—still weird to think like that—she hadn't been able to meet his gaze; now, she *truly* couldn't meet this gaze. This man was Alpha. *Her* Alpha.

And how strange was *that*?

"Doing okay, Avery?" Gideon asked, his voice deep. He looked between the three of them and raised a brow. No doubt he had an inkling of what had happened the night before. Considering they were all wolves and had enhanced senses, she had a feeling there would be no hiding certain things from anyone anymore.

"I am."

"Good. If you need anything and Parker and Brandon can't help you for some reason, you find me or one of the Brentwoods. We'll help you. I'm sorry you came into the Pack this way, but we're still grateful you're one of us."

She opened her mouth to say something but was cut off by a woman's yell.

"Parker!"

A woman with long, flowing hair and a silk and lace dress ran toward Parker, leaping into his arms before anyone had a chance to wonder what the hell was going on. Parker let out an *umph* and seemed to automatically hold out his arms to catch the woman. He looked over at Gideon, and his eyes narrowed before he set the pretty young thing down.

Avery paused that line of thinking, annoyed with herself for feeling even the slightest amount of jealousy. She had no real claim on Parker, nor did she know who might lay within his past. Just because they'd had one night together and were potential mates didn't mean she had the right to be petty about a pretty woman with long legs.

Maybe she was his sister, Isabelle.

Then the woman kissed Parker right on the lips, and Brandon had to put a hand on Avery's shoulder so she didn't move forward.

Holy hell. What was wrong with her? She'd *never* acted like this before. She prided herself on the fact that she could usually hold in her emotions and control them to a certain extent. She'd been forced to do that at a young age because if she felt *too* much, she could bring on a vision when she wasn't ready. Maybe this was what the men had meant about her wolf pushing at her emotions. There was this new...being inside her, and she had to learn to live with it, or she'd go insane.

Avery let out a breath, trying to control the wolf inside her. It wasn't easy since all she wanted to do was use her new claws to slash that too sweet smile off the young maiden's face. Yeah, okay, that was bitchy, and she needed to get a grip. There was seriously something wrong with her if her jealousy was this high after just one night with the man.

"Tatiana," Parker said in a soft voice. "What are you doing here?"

"She *looks* like a Tatiana," Brie mumbled from Avery's side, and Avery bit her lip to stop from laughing. She hadn't even noticed that the other woman had waddled up beside them and, apparently, Brie was of a similar mindset as Avery.

"Hush," Avery whispered back. "We shouldn't be catty."

"And you should probably speak lower since we're wolves," Brandon added in an almost inaudible whisper.

Tatiana beamed at him. "I was just so worried after you fell ill in our Pack, that I asked my Alpha if I could come visit to ensure you didn't need anything. I helped you recover, after all. Your Healer might want to ask me questions. I went to the Redwood den first, but the sentries wouldn't permit me entrance. Instead, they told me you were here."

Brandon put a hand on Avery's shoulder again, and she let out a breath. If she didn't get a handle on the raging emotions inside her, she wouldn't be able to breathe. It hurt that this woman from Parker's past seemed to know more about Parker than she did. Yes, she'd met him only a short time ago, but they'd already done so much together that she couldn't quite keep her thoughts and feelings in order.

Gideon cleared his throat. "Why don't the two of you talk since you indeed know her? Her Alpha called right as she arrived, so she's here with his permission."

"Of course, I am," Tatiana said, her accent soft, her head lowered. "I wouldn't dream of disobeying my Alpha."

Avery pressed her lips together and didn't dare look at Brie since she could feel the other woman's body shaking with leashed laughter.

"I'm going to take Avery to get something to eat and show her around the den," Brie said finally, cutting into the awkward silence.

Gideon glowered. "You shouldn't be on your feet at all."

Brie rolled her eyes, not looking like a submissive wolf in the least. "Okay, your highness, I'll be good and just walk Avery to our place so I can feed her. She's my new wolf, too, your Alphaness. I need to ensure that she's well taken care of."

Avery leaned into Brandon as Gideon stormed over, a mixture of worry, exasperation, and intense love in his eyes. She would have felt sorry for Brie for dealing with the giant of a man, but the smaller woman just smiled sweetly before going on her tiptoes to kiss his chin.

"I'll be fine, Gideon. Go talk to Brandon like you wanted to and leave Avery to me."

Avery's heart clutched just a fraction at the sight of the big bad Alpha doting on his mate, but she didn't dare say anything. The man was seriously scary to everyone else, and there was no way she would get in the middle of that. However, going off with Brie sounded like a fine idea since she really didn't think she could hold her wolf back for much longer when it came to Tatiana.

"Food sounds wonderful to me," Avery said honestly. She'd eaten already that morning, but she was still a little hungry. The men had told her that her metabolism would change, and that she'd need more food than she was used to, but the hunger mixed with jealousy and uncertainty wasn't something she liked nor was it something she wanted to think about.

Parker gave her a strange look, and Brandon slid his hand down over her side, squeezing her hip. As always, she couldn't read either of them. Parker might be the one who spoke more, but she didn't know what he was trying to tell her then. As for Brandon, he was as closed-off emotionally as ever. Considering he was the Omega of the Pack, she wasn't sure what to think about that.

"Good," Brie said quickly, taking Avery's hand. "Have fun, boys." And with that, Brie pulled Avery behind her, leaving the others where they stood. For such a pregnant wolf, who apparently needed to be kept off her feet, the woman sure was strong.

When they were out of hearing range, Avery finally let out a small laugh. "You know, I don't know if that was subtle enough."

Brie waved her off, a small smile on her face. "Oh, whatever. You, Brandon, and Parker might not be mated yet, but there's an air about the three of you. That other wolf isn't going to get in the middle of that. Parker just needs to not be so *nice* and tell the girl what's what. But since he *is* nice, he'll want privacy to do it, so he doesn't embarrass her."

Avery shook her head as Brie led her into the Alpha's home. "How can you be so sure?"

Brie smiled widely, her eyes bright. "Because I know Parker. He's been part of my life since I was a baby and has always been there. I was born into the Redwoods, but he didn't come along until he was eight or so. He and my cousin Charlotte were the older two cousins running the herd. Finn and I came next, then Micah and the rest of them."

Avery shook her head, taking a seat at the kitchen bar so Brie would do the same. The woman looked ready to pop, and she might say she was doing just fine, but Avery didn't want to endure the Alpha's wrath should any harm come to the woman in Avery's care.

"There sure are a lot of you Redwoods."

Brie snorted. "Yep, and we keep mating with Talons. That means Gideon and Kade, the Redwood Alpha, are constantly having to deal with one another. It gets a bit growly, but one day, I have a feeling we'll be one large Pack with two Alphas. There's just so much crossover it's hard to keep the lines straight."

"I'm having a hard time keeping the *names* straight, let alone the bonds."

Brie reached out and gripped Avery's hand, the strength within the woman calming her. Avery didn't understand it, but her wolf was at peace next to Brie.

"What..."

"I'm a submissive wolf, Avery. My wolf soothes those dominants around me. And though your wolf is still finding her place, I have a feeling you'll eventually find yourself higher in the dominance scale than you might have thought. Both Parker and Brandon are dominant, as well, so the three of you will be a force."

Avery pulled away, slightly shaken and not wanting to talk about her wolf. Not yet. "We aren't mated. There wasn't even a true pull or whatever you guys call it. Brandon said the bonds are different."

Brie frowned but nodded. "He spoke to us about it on the phone earlier. I don't know what that means for our people, but we'll overcome. We've conquered so much."

She let out a breath. "I was born in a time of war, grew up in a time of peace." She rested her hands over the swell of her belly. "Now, my child will be born in a time of war. But no matter what happens, life continues. Don't you see? We will survive, even if our ways have to evolve with the world in order to do so. The three of you haven't bonded yet, and there is no mark between you, but you *sense* the place where a bond could go."

Avery swallowed hard. "How do you know that?"

Brie shook her head. "I'm your Alpha female. I might not be the most dominant wolf in the Pack, far from it, but I'm still the Alpha's mate. I can sense when my wolves are at the precipice, looking down at what could be their future or their failure. You're not mated to the two of them yet, but you've only just begun to know them. Take the time to truly understand what mating could mean, or at least get a sense of it. And when you're ready, when you've bonded, we will figure out the lines and Pack loyalties. We've done it in the past, and we will do it again. But for now, take the time you have."

The only problem, Avery worried, was that she wasn't sure how much time her men had left.

CHAPTER 10

BRANDON WATCHED Avery walk away with Brie, a frown on his face. He didn't like the way she'd fled the situation, but he couldn't blame her. He didn't like how his wolf reacted to this Tatiana either. However, he'd had over a century to learn to control his wolf, while Avery hadn't even had a full week. This…jealousy of his was a new and unwanted emotion that he wanted no part of, though. He'd felt it before, of course, but due to other people's emotions rather than his own.

He'd never wanted someone enough in his long years to truly feel anything other than a mild annoyance when others touched what he thought of as his. Of course, this was the first time he'd found *his*, so he wasn't sure what to do about anything anymore.

Parker glared at Avery's retreating back before looking

toward Brandon. He tilted his head in question, but Brandon didn't say anything. Anyone with the nose of a wolf would be able to scent both Brandon and Avery all over Parker's skin. They might not be mated, but their night together was fresh enough that the scent layer was still there. One day soon, he hoped, the imprint would never leave—would be so deeply embedded within each of their skins that no one would doubt who belonged to whom. But for now, Brandon would have to trust Parker with this new development.

But, as always for a Brentwood, trust didn't come easily.

"Parker, you can take your friend over to the clearing near the sentry gate. Brandon and I will be with the others when you're through."

Gideon gave both Brandon and Parker pointed looks before walking away, leaving Brandon standing there with his hands in his pockets, feeling slightly off. Once again, he was the brother put in the awkward position and not knowing what to do, so he nodded at Parker before turning away to follow his brother and Alpha.

"Brandon," Parker called out.

Brandon froze before looking over his shoulder at the man he craved. "Yeah?"

"I won't be long," Parker said smoothly. Brandon

didn't miss the way Tatiana's shoulders stiffened at those words. Nor did he miss the heat in Parker's gaze.

He nodded before silently following Gideon, his mind on so many things and yet not focusing on one thing long enough for it to really matter.

They were near the tree line when Gideon finally spoke. "She says she's just a friend. One who helped heal Parker when he was ill."

There was a question there, though Gideon hadn't voiced it. "I know he was ill," Brandon said after a moment. "But I think it's his story to tell." Though he hadn't known about this Tatiana and what she might have meant to Parker. The Voice of the Wolves had come home for many reasons, one of them being that he was in dire need of a mate. If Tatiana had been another potential, he wouldn't have come back.

And as long as Brandon kept thinking that, he would be fine.

"He came to stay with us because he said it would be safer for his family if he were here. He also said he wouldn't be a danger to the Talons, and I still believe him." A pause. "Whatever happened in the European Pack must have been enough that he felt the need to run from the family that has always been there for him."

Brandon blew out a breath before stopping to lean

against the trunk of a large tree. Gideon leaned against the one across from him, folding his arms over his large chest.

"I don't know what we're doing," Brandon said softly.

"Of course, you don't," Gideon said with a dry laugh. "You're in the middle of the mating urge, and you didn't even have your wolf around to tell you that you should be going that way to begin with. You're not only going through a crazy time in your life during one of the craziest of times in our history, but you're forging a new trail as you do it. It's not going to be easy, but you're a fucking Brentwood. You're going to figure it out."

Brandon stared at his brother, his Alpha. Everything the man said sounded so easy coming from Gideon's lips, and yet Brandon knew it was anything but.

"How am I supposed to trust the journey, trust the moon goddess, when I feel as though the connection we should have is gone?"

Gideon shook his head. "It's changed, maybe not completely gone. My mating bond with Brie hasn't altered, and I have a feeling the other mating bonds haven't changed either, or we'd have heard about it. But what *has* changed is how we find our mates. Maybe there are no such things as true potentials anymore, and we make our own fate? Or maybe we'll have harder times in the future, but we'll persevere." Gideon's gaze was bleak. "If we don't, then I'm not sure what else we can do."

"We fight," Max said as he made his way to the clearing where Gideon and Brandon stood.

Max grinned after he said it and moved out of the way so the other males in their family who stood behind him could join the group. Of all the brothers and cousins in Brandon's family, Max was the one that smiled the most. He wasn't the youngest of them, but he had that carefree air. He was Mitchell's brother, Brandon's cousin. And because there was that distinction, Brandon had a feeling Mitchell had shielded his younger brother from the worst of their childhood. Though Max had been through his own hell, he'd come out of it with a brighter attitude than the others, as if that had been his coping mechanism instead of the brooding distance so many of them favored.

"We've been fighting," Mitchell grumbled. He was their Beta, and as such, knew the ins and outs of the daily needs of the Pack.

While the Heir and Alpha positions always went to the firstborn son of the eldest of the family, the other positions could go to any of the Pack members. Statistically, the Enforcer, Omega, Healer, and Beta went to other family members, but not always. And while for most Packs, men held those positions, there were more women in each upcoming generation. In fact, the newest generation of Redwood hierarchy had more females than ever before. And for some reason, Brandon had a feeling the

Talons would be following in their footsteps soon with Gideon and Brie's child. The couple had chosen to keep the gender secret from everyone but Walker, their Healer, and the man wasn't saying a damn thing—no matter how high the pool got. Most assumed it would be a boy, as the Alpha *always* had a boy first so that child would one day wear the mantle of Heir once he was ready—or in some cases when the Alpha died unexpectedly. Yet times were changing rapidly, so Brandon wasn't sure of anything anymore. One day, Gideon and Brie's child would be Heir, taking the burden from Ryder's shoulders, and eventually, maybe even in a century or two if the goddess were willing, that child would be Alpha.

"We'll continue to fight," Kameron said with a growl. Brandon's fellow triplet and the Pack Enforcer growled with each word he bit out these days. Brandon didn't know what was going on with his brother, but knew he'd have to find out soon. All the Brentwoods had long ago learned to shield their heavier emotions from Brandon, and he'd given them privacy for as long as he could stomach it. Soon, though, he'd have to find a way to help them—before it was too late.

He was the Omega. It was his calling to help those in need—even if they didn't want it.

Walker sighed as he sank down to the ground at Brandon's feet, weariness in his features. While most of the

Pack had healed from the last battle with Montag, not everyone was out of the woods yet. There was only so much their brother could do as Healer, and some things just took time.

Ryder sat next to Walker, a frown on his face. "I have a feeling the fighting won't last much longer, not with how close we are to the breaking point." He rubbed the back of his neck. "I just had a lovely meeting with the Coven, and they're ready to mount an assault if any more of their witches are taken into custody for questioning."

"Fuck," Mitchell growled. "I thought you were making sure they listened to us and worked with us rather than doing their own thing."

Ryder flipped him off. "I'm mated to a damn witch, but I'm *not* a damn witch—their words. They'll only take what I have to say so far. And, hell, because we have so many young and we're not just one Pack, but representing *many*, our hands seemed tied to the outside world who think they know us."

"They don't know us at all," Mitchell whispered. There was something in his cousin's tone that made Brandon look over and focus. For the second time in just a few short days he saw behind the mask and almost fell to his knees.

And *fuck*, the pain the other man held inside…

It was as if a raging inferno engulfed the other man

daily before ramping up again to burn the flesh from his bones and the ache from his heart. Brandon honestly had no idea what had happened in Mitchell's past to cause him this much pain, but if he could help in any way, he would.

So he did the only thing he could do as an Omega and tried to take at least a fraction of the pain within him.

It burned. The agony arching up his spine so quickly that tears sprang to his eyes. His wolf howled and twisted the emotion around itself before letting it dissipate through the bonds Brandon held.

Mitchell's gaze shot to his, pure rage spiraling through the other man's eyes. "Stop."

And with that one word, Mitchell stood up, tightly locking down his emotions before storming away, leaving the others in mid-conversation.

Brandon let out a shaky breath, his already weakening body that much weaker. He knew without a bond he might not be able to help anyone soon, but he wasn't about to rush Avery and Parker when he still had a little bit of time.

But he wasn't sure Mitchell had as much.

"He never asks for help," Max said softly, breaking the tense silence. "No matter how much I try to annoy him into yelling at me and spilling his guts, he doesn't ask for help. I don't know what happened, but thank you for taking some of his pain. He won't thank you, but I will."

And that was why Brandon loved Max so much. The man put everyone else ahead of himself, even to his detriment.

Gideon cursed under his breath. "Our family's breaking again, yet, as always, I need to push that aside and worry about the health and safety of the Pack as a whole. What kind of Alpha does that make me that I have to worry about the humans attacking our people rather than what secrets our family holds so close to the vest that it's destroying them slowly day by day?"

"An Alpha with a group of people around him that he trusts with more than his life," Ryder said simply, though his statement was anything but simple. "You trust us to make sure we're doing our part. That's the sign of a healthy Pack, even if it doesn't look like it. I know you want to go claws out at the humans for hurting us again and again, and each time they attack our den, we defeat them. But it's taking its toll."

"But we're going to win," Brandon added softly.

"Because there isn't another option." Kameron's voice once again held the hint of a growl. "We have the wolves we need in Washington. This battle isn't fought with tooth and claw, at least not right now. We aren't politicians, and they know it. But others are, and they're the ones fighting with words and on paper. I'd rather smash my fist into someone's face than have to do a speech about how wolves are people too, but that's where we're at. And when this McMaster makes another move and attacks our den like Montag did, then we'll fight. We'll fight because they've looked at our Pack and decided we're the ones to take down first. If we fall, then other Packs will have to take our place."

"It's not just us," Gideon corrected. "We have the Redwoods, as well." He glared. "I thought we'd have the Aspens, but now that we killed one of their missing wolves, they've decided to hold back on help."

Brandon's gaze shot up. "What? They aren't actually blaming us?"

Gideon cursed. "They're blaming both the Redwoods and the Talons. It doesn't matter that their rogue attacked us first. It seems this wolf had been missing for over a year."

The hairs on the back of Brandon's neck stood on end. "Who had him all that time?"

Gideon's eyes glowed gold, his wolf at the surface. "That's what I intend to find out. Because all of this screams that there's a ploy at work."

"Montag's cages were all empty when we got to the compound," Ryder bit out. Montag had been torturing wolves for who knew how long to find out the shifters' secrets. But even with the man's death, it didn't mean everyone was safe.

"We all knew the general had to have an accomplice," Gideon said. "And I have a feeling we're watching him at work every time he smiles to the cameras."

"McMaster." Brandon let out a growl of his own. "What is the senator playing at?"

Gideon shook his head. "I don't know yet, but I intend to find out. Because our Pack won't be safe until the humans stop looking at us as predators on the loose, but rather as shifters with rights of our own."

Brandon fisted his hands at his side, aware that the time would come when they'd either be seen as safer in the eyes of humans, or all would truly be lost. Shifters might be able to change into animals, but that didn't *make* them animals. If the humans didn't realize that…well, then it would be the end of the Packs themselves.

Their wards were failing. Their people were too confined within the dens after years of living in secret. Hate crimes were skyrocketing against those the humans thought were different—even if they weren't a witch or a wolf.

They were on the edge of a mass shift in what it meant to be a part of humanity.

And Brandon wasn't sure if any of them would survive to see the outcome.

CHAPTER 11

PARKER PEELED Tatiana off his side, annoyed, tired, and emotionally wrung out. He didn't have it in him to deal with...whatever this was right then, but he knew he didn't have a choice. They were now relatively alone except for the two sentries who stood by on guard. Neither he nor Tatiana was Pack, so Parker didn't blame the two guards one bit for staying near.

He'd rather be with Avery and Brandon, working out exactly what was going on between them, but, apparently, that wasn't going to happen right now.

"Tatiana," he said in a clear voice. "What are you doing here?"

She frowned. "I came to see if you were well after your illness." Her voice held the slight lilting accent of her place of birth, but he didn't find it tempting. She was a beautiful woman who would make someone very happy in mating one day, but she was not *his* woman.

"I'm doing much better," he lied. It wasn't fully a lie since meeting Brandon and Avery had put new life within him, but he wasn't recovered yet. The dizziness and pain spells still attacked him out of nowhere, and according to Tatiana's elders, he wouldn't heal fully until he found his mate.

He hadn't taken them at their word, of course, but had gone to one of his own elders, Emeline, to ask what she knew. She was one of the oldest wolves in the Redwood Pack, but since she'd newly mated a wolf about thirty years ago named Noah, she also was more down to earth than many of the otherworldly elders he'd met in his travels.

"I've heard of the spear of the first hunter," Emeline had said when he'd given her his secrets. He'd kept everything so close to the vest, but he'd needed to tell *someone*. He knew she'd tell her mate, of course, but Noah wouldn't tell another soul unless it was harmful to the Pack.

"What do you know of it?" Parker had asked.

"All I know is that the spear was the one that killed the wolf during the man's hunt. The moon goddess broke the blade off the tip of the spear and threw it deep into the forest." Emeline had smiled at him softly. "This is all legend, Parker, you know this. But you're also of the line of the hunters, and as the moon goddess talks to us on occasion, we know that legends are born of truth. I don't know how the spear ended up in the hands of a Pack so far away, but it could be true. You see, long ago, when the first hunter came back to his people, he made more wolves. It was a viscous time, as you know, making so many wolves, but his own wolf needed a Pack of its own so he would not live so long alone. I don't know if the moon goddess planned that, but she has her reasons for everything, so I wouldn't be surprised. The first hunter made three wolves at first, using his three closest friends."

"And then the three men made more and so on," Parker had continued for her. "I remember this story now. My mother told it to me as it was told to her."

"She's of the first line, as well, so she would want your history to be carried on. The sons of the first set of wolves eventually moved away to create more Packs. From there, we now have the Packs within our country and around the world. It could be that one of those sons took the spear with him to Europe and formed a Pack there. We might not ever know. But if you're this sick from a disease that only hurts your line, I would think this could actually be true. And I might not know exactly how to heal you, but I do know that mating bonds are the strongest bonds there are, even stronger than that of an Alpha with his people. If anything can soothe the ache and heal the heart, it's a mating bond."

Parker had said his thanks after they'd finished talking and moved out of the Redwood den the next day. He hadn't known he'd find his potential mates so quickly, but he'd known he couldn't risk hurting his family.

But before he could deal with any of that, he needed to make sure Tatiana knew exactly what was going on.

"I'm glad to hear you're better," the woman said with a small smile.

"You could have called," Parker said, slightly annoyed. "You didn't need to fly across a freaking ocean to see me. What is really going on?"

She sighed and pressed her lips together. "I thought…I thought there was a connection between us."

He held back a curse. "There wasn't, Tatiana. You know this." And while things with finding potential mates might have changed, Parker would have felt *some* sort of attraction if she were indeed his intended. He knew at least that much remained the same, as was evidenced by what had happened between him, Brandon, and Avery.

She closed her eyes, and he felt like a jerk but he couldn't help it. She wasn't his mate, and while she might be attracted to him, she was still so young when it came to emotions and the way the world worked. Why her Alpha had even let her come to a strange den on her own, he didn't know, but he'd be having a talk with the other man soon. He hadn't liked him to begin with, and now, he really didn't.

"I found my mates," he said after a moment.

"Mates?" she said with a smile that confused him. "Truly? You found more than one?"

"Yes..."

"The two that were here and looked like they wanted to hurt me for daring to touch you?" She sighed. "You are truly blessed to find these mates. I thought...well, I thought there might be something between you and me, but I was clearly wrong. Please forgive me for making things awkward. And I hope I didn't harm the bond you hold with them."

Off-kilter, he didn't mention that he hadn't actually bonded with Avery and Brandon yet.

"I also came for another reason," she said quickly, making his wolf perk up to attention. "My Alpha does not want to become public, even though many humans around the den have already guessed what we are. There will be no hiding soon, but he doesn't see that. I want to help fight on the front lines. I'm a stronger fighter than people give me credit for because of the way I dress and how small I am, but I don't want to go into the next century—if I'm blessed to make it out of the war alive—and know I didn't do everything I could to protect my people. My Alpha sent me this way because he didn't want to deal with my whining anymore, and that is fine. I will do what I can to make sure that *all* wolves have a fighting chance." She winced. "I kind of used you to get out here. And for that, I'm sorry."

Parker blinked at her before barking out a laugh. "You knew we weren't mates and yet you told him we might be so you could leave your Pack and head out here to help us fight?"

She bit her lip. "Well, I didn't know if we could be or not. I've never felt a mate before, and for all I knew, you could be it. So that *was* the truth, if not all of it."

He shook his head. "Okay, then. I guess I need to see what Gideon has to say about that." He paused. "No, Kade. Let's go to *my* Alpha and see what he has to say." That way, she wouldn't be anywhere near his two mates just in case there were any issues. He had a feeling Tatiana wanted to do more with her life than be the soft-spoken aide of the elders, but he still needed to be careful.

After all, every wolf was more than they seemed—this young maiden from a far-off land included.

By the time he got back to the Talon den, his

head ached, but at least Tatiana was safe with the Redwoods. They had cautiously welcomed her, all the while giving him a look that said they would be expecting him to explain in full later. And he knew they were right to worry. He hadn't been honest with them about what had happened, and now that was going to bite him in the ass. Brandon and Avery knew, but not his parents or Pack. That would have to change soon, and he had a feeling Tatiana would change it for him if he weren't careful.

He was on his way back to Brandon's when his phone buzzed. With a sigh, he answered and kept walking.

"What do you want, Blake?"

"So, this girl just shows up out of the blue with big eyes and long, flowing hair and you say you had nothing to do with her? I mean, she followed you across the damn ocean, and you're just leaving her with us? And don't even get me started on the whole thing where she says she healed you because I'm about to kick your ass for failing to mention that you almost fucking died over there."

Parker pinched the bridge of his nose, thankful that Blake was on the phone rather than in front of him. He wasn't sure he would be able to deal with his brother face-to-face at the moment.

"I didn't touch her, and I'll talk about everything else soon. I promise. Now, go be the good son and take care of Mom and Dad while I deal with my own problems."

"You're an idiot, big brother. You're always the good son."

"I love you, too, Blake." He smiled despite everything going on around him because his brother could always make him laugh.

"Love you, big brother. Now, go get it on with those two wolves that you're going to mate, and let me see what I can do with this sweet new wolf in our den."

Parker barked out a laugh and hung up, aware that Tatiana was probably going to end up in over her head if Blake had set his sights on her. He'd just made it into Brandon's house when the scent of home, heat, and pine surrounded him. He turned as Avery and Brandon walked into the house, their faces carefully blank.

Fuck. He'd been the one to make them hurt, and he needed to fix it. What they had was fragile as hell right now, and just one mistake could shatter it all.

"Tatiana is with the Redwoods," Parker blurted out. Avery raised a brow, and he held back a curse. As usual, Brandon didn't do a damn thing but look at him, his emotions locked down tightly. "She's from my past, not my present, and definitely not my future." He cursed again at the look on Avery's face. "Tatiana and I were never together, but she *was* there to help me heal enough to come back to the den. She's a sweet girl, but not for me, and not my mate. I'm sorry if her being here hurt you in any way."

Avery winced before coming up to him and wrapping her arms around his waist. "I'm sorry, I'm acting like a jealous girlfriend instead of being an adult about the fact that, hey, you do have a past and have probably had sex with other people."

"I never had sex with Tatiana. Not even close," he interjected.

"Be that as it may, my wolf is riding me hard." She looked back and scrunched her face. "At least, I think that's what's happening. I'm not sure *what* is going on exactly, but I'm really new to this whole thing and not acting like myself."

Brandon chose that moment to move forward and place his hand on Avery's back. "I think we're all feeling the mating heat, and our emotions are running a little high right now." He looked directly into Parker's eyes. "And I do believe you. It was just a little shocking to see her jump into your arms after our night together."

"But that's on us, not you," Avery added. "And we'll do better." She looked at Brandon. "Right?"

Brandon smiled softly before kissing the tip of her nose. Parker's wolf perked up, enjoying their interaction. "We'll try."

Avery snorted, and Parker squeezed her hip. "It's so

weird that I'm perfectly fine with you two getting it on, but the idea of anyone else near one of you makes me want to use my claws."

Parker shook his head. "Not weird at all. Triads aren't that much different from other relationships. Instead of two, there are three, so there shouldn't be jealousy *within* the relationship."

"And even though it's a relationship of three, there are also connections between each of us as pairs," Brandon added. "That's why some of the triads I know are the strongest matings I've ever brushed up against. It takes more effort, and far more communication for it to work, but in the end…if this mating is what we want, then we'll thrive."

Parker swallowed hard, his wolf at the forefront. "I…I hope that's what we do."

Avery looked between them. "I'm not ready for that kind of bond yet," she whispered softly. "I know you both need it, but I need time to get to know you guys."

Parker leaned down and brushed a kiss over her lips. "Take your time, wolf of mine." He'd rather fade away than hurt the woman in his arms, and he needed her to know that.

Brandon opened his mouth to speak at that instant but froze, his eyes going glassy as he pitched forward. Parker gripped the man who would be his mate by the hips and caught him before he fell.

"What is it?" Parker growled. "A ward flare again?"

Brandon shook his head, his face pale, his skin clammy. Avery cupped Brandon's cheek and looked into his eyes while Parker did his best to keep the man steady.

"What's wrong? Do we need to get Walker?"

Once again, Brandon shook his head before taking a deep breath. "It wasn't the wards," he croaked out.

Parker cursed and gently nudged Avery back before lifting Brandon into his arms. Brandon clearly wasn't at full-strength because he wrapped his arms around Parker's neck and leaned in while Parker walked them to the couch, Avery behind them. He sat down, Brandon in his lap, and Avery at their side. Parker might not be at full-strength either, but he was still wolf enough to lift Brandon without straining himself.

"What was it, then?" Avery asked. She was on her knees beside them, running her hands down their arms.

Brandon let out a long breath. "I'm having these dreams. Maybe visions? I don't know, but they knock me for a loop each time. I just don't know. It's like I'm seeing the past, but it makes no sense."

Avery's eyes widened, and Parker blinked. He hadn't been expecting that at all.

"So, let me get this straight," Parker said after a moment, "Avery sees the future. You see the past. And it looks like I'm stuck here in the present." He looked between the two of them. "What the fuck does this mean?"

He didn't have an answer to that, but he had a feeling the question was only the beginning.

CHAPTER 12

AVERY WASHED her face the next morning, her brain still a little fuzzy from sleep. After the three of them had talked on the couch, they'd all been exhausted so they climbed into Brandon's large bed and fell asleep fully clothed and wrapped around each other in a puppy pile. If she hadn't had so many other life-altering changes recently, she'd have found that weird. Instead, she rolled with it because dwelling for too long on things she couldn't change would only hurt her in the end.

She'd also had a vision that morning as soon as she'd woken up, one she couldn't quite decipher. Her stomach roiled as she remembered what she'd seen. There had been blood everywhere, screams and shouts surrounding them as they fought an unseen enemy. Her hands shook, and she ran them over her face, trying to remember each moment, each breath. Shadows surrounded her, pulling at her hair, her skin, her clothes.

She'd seen a man fighting another hand-to-hand, and people screaming around them. Pain radiated through her as she saw someone she loved hit the ground, but she didn't know if they were alive or dead. She wasn't *there* in the vision, but watching it from afar. She couldn't be sure if she were the one fighting alongside them, or someone too late to do anything but scream in agony. She tried to see more, but it was all so hazy, she hadn't been able to figure out what any of it meant. She hated visions like that. Ones where they didn't tell her anything, and explaining them to another person only led to more questions and confusion.

Later today, she had her first training session with Kameron, and she was oddly looking forward to it. The Enforcer didn't always personally train wolves to fight, but since she was living with his triplet, Kameron had taken a special interest in her. She wasn't quite sure how she felt about that, but she'd get over it like she'd gotten over so much recently. Either way, though, she would learn how to protect herself now that she was on the other side of things. She'd taken a few self-defense classes back in college and could handle herself with her camera, but that didn't mean much when she had to learn how to control her wolf at the same time she controlled her limbs.

"You doing okay in there?" Brandon asked from the other side of the door. Just hearing his voice sent delicious shivers down her body, and she had to grip the edge of the sink to stay upright.

Parker had left early that morning after kissing them both senseless since he wanted to meet with his parents before their shifts. She was truly happy he was finally doing that since she knew from what he'd said that he was really close with his family. She'd grown up in a family of lies and secrets, and she didn't want that for anyone else.

Instead of answering Brandon, she opened the door and smiled. He looked all sexy and rumpled since he hadn't showered yet. Instead, he'd made them all breakfast—something other than a protein shake—and the whole thing had been truly domestic. If she thought about how much her life had changed in such a short time, she'd run screaming, so she purposely didn't think about it.

Brandon reached out and traced her jaw with his finger. "You didn't answer."

She leaned into his touch, her wolf brushing up against her skin lazily. "I'm good. Just taking a slow morning since Kameron is planning on whipping me into shape later."

Brandon's eyes darkened. "I'll be there, as well. He won't hurt you."

She rolled her eyes. *Men.* "I'll probably get a little bruised. You don't need to go all growly wolf over it."

Brandon's nostril's flared. "I can't help that."

She patted his chest before leaning forward and kissing his chin. "I know. But I'm still going to call you out on it."

He wrapped his hands around her waist and pulled her closer. The hard ridge of his cock pressed against her belly, and she groaned, her panties already wet from just that one touch. "Good." Then he crushed his mouth to hers.

She moaned, deepening the kiss. His hands massaged her butt, gripping her tightly. She slid her hands around so she could scrape her fingers down his back, needing him more than she ever thought possible.

She was about to wrap her leg around his waist so her clit would press right against the line of his dick, when he abruptly pulled away, panting. He turned so his back was to her and he bent forward, hands on his knees.

"What is it?" She moved to stand in front of him, her hands shaking. "What's wrong?" She hated that both her men were in pain, and the only thing she could do about it was either stand back and watch, or tie her soul to them forever. And while the latter was looking more and more appealing, both her men had both said it might be too soon for her wolf. That many changes and bonds introduced to her system at once might hurt her. And that wasn't even considering the emotional impact of finding herself mated to not one, but *two* dominant wolves when she'd truly thought she would be alone for the rest of her life.

"Just a small ward flare." He stood up then, inhaling deeply through his nose. "I'm sorry for ruining the moment."

She shook her head and wrapped herself round him, needing his heartbeat under her ear so she could calm her racing pulse. "There's no such thing as a small ward flare."

He hugged her close and kissed the top of her head. "No, I guess there isn't." He paused, and his next words were so bleak she had to blink tears from her eyes. "The wards are failing, Avery. With every flare, our protections come closer and closer to falling down. And no matter what the witches do, they aren't strong enough alone to keep them up. And it's not just us, this is happening in every Pack we have contact with."

Avery pressed a kiss to his chest. "And once the wards fall..."

She didn't finish her sentence. There was no point when they both knew the outcome. Their people would be truly vulnerable to whatever McMaster and the others had planned.

Brandon held her close, and she tipped her head up, needing his kiss. He pressed his mouth to hers, and she licked at him, needing him more than she could say.

When he pulled back, he cupped her face with his hands. "I want you, Avery."

She licked her lips. "I want you, too. Is this okay without Parker here?" She'd never been in a triad before, and frankly, had never thought about how things would work.

Brandon smiled. "I told you this last night, remember? Each relationship is a duo within the trio. There will be times with just you and me, times with you and Parker."

She pressed her legs together, delicious warmth licking at her with just the thought. "And you and Parker, too, right?"

Brandon bit her lip. "Hell, yeah, me and Parker, too."

"That sounds like a plan because I have a feeling once you and he are done with me not only separately but together, I might need a break." She winked. "At least my lady bits will."

Brandon threw back his head and laughed. "Hate to break it to you, babe, but I have a feeling you're the one who's going to wear us out, not the other way around."

She gripped the edge of his shirt. "Prove it."

Brandon's eyes glowed gold. "That, I can do." And he crushed his mouth to hers, his body shaking.

Avery wrapped her arms around him, needing him inside her, around her, *everything* to do with her...*now*. She slid her hands up his back, under his shirt, needing to feel his skin. She'd never been this tactile before, never this in need of skin-to-skin, and she didn't know if it was because of her wolf, or because of Parker and Brandon themselves. In the end, it didn't matter because she just needed *them*.

Brandon picked her up as if she weighed nothing, and she wrapped her legs around his waist, needing him more than she could say.

"I was going to go slow," Brandon growled. "Take my time with you so I could enjoy every inch of you, but I don't think I can."

She licked her lips before arching her back, pressing her core against the hard length of him. "Then let me do the work for a bit," she said.

He raised both brows. "And how are you going to do that?"

"I have my ways." She wiggled down, and he let her go. When she went to kneel in front of him, he groaned before reaching over the back of the couch to grab a throw pillow.

"As much as I want your mouth on me, I'd rather you not hurt your knees in the process."

This man was going to kill her with more than orgasms, and she was really okay with that.

"Can you take off your shirt when you do this?" he asked with a smile. "I'd like to see your pretty breasts when you take me into your mouth.

Seriously. This man.

She quickly took off her clothes, leaving her bare. She'd have kept the pants on, but she might as well get fully naked. His answering smile told her she'd done the perfect thing. He trailed his hands down her body, stopping to cup her breasts and pinch her nipples between his fingers before helping her kneel down on the pillow.

Brandon stripped off his shirt as she undid his pants, pulling out the length of him with her hand. He was wide enough that her fingers didn't touch when she wrapped them around the base, and she licked her lips. He'd been inside her with this thing, and frankly, she was surprised she'd been able to walk afterward. He ran his hand through her hair, and she looked up at him as she licked the tip. He shuddered, his eyes growing dark even as the gold ring around his iris glowed, telling her he was both wolf and man, primal, *hers*.

She sucked on the head, using her tongue to play with him as she explored his feel and salty taste. He made a guttural groan, and she figured he must like what she was doing. When she took more of him in, she assumed she wouldn't be able to swallow him all, so she used her hands to make sure she could at least touch all of him at the same time.

When she began to bob her head, his hips moved fractionally, tiny thrusts in and out of her mouth. She was still the one in control—barely—and he was doing his best not to choke her. Everything this man did was for the care of others, and she wanted him to know that he was appreciated. So she played with the skin behind his balls, using her nails to scratch lightly. Brandon let out a shout, his hands tightening in her hair.

"I'm going to come." She tried to keep him in her mouth, but he was stronger. So she leaned back and groaned as he came on her breasts, the act much sexier than she thought possible.

Brandon cursed. "As fucking hot as that was, baby, I got you all dirty."

She came to her feet with his help and kissed him. "Then get me clean so you can fuck me." He was in and out of the kitchen in a blink, using a wet cloth to wipe her with one hand, and using his other hand to rub small circles over her clit. She started to pant, his calloused fingers working her so quickly that she was already about to come, and she felt like they hadn't even started yet.

"Top or bottom?" he asked, and she laughed.

"I love that we get to ask that question every time we have sex, no matter which one of us it is."

Brandon kissed her again, leaving her melting at his feet. "I like that you always answer and don't give me a weird look."

She rolled her eyes. "I like sex. I *really* like sex with you. I'm not going to act all dainty about having your cock in me. I mean, I can if we want to play it that way for a night, but what I really want is to ride you while you sit down because that means you get to play with my ass at the same time." She winked. "Then…"

"Then I want you on your side so I can fuck you from behind that way."

Her eyes widened. "I've never tried that."

Brandon kissed her again. "Then I'd better show you." Brandon took her hand and led her around the couch. He sat down, his cock hard and sticking straight up. "Hop on, baby."

She wiggled her hips, loving that they could joke even as they made themselves come. Sex was serious, but it could also be fun. Finding the right mix was what made what they were doing perfect.

He held out a hand, and she took it, swinging one leg over his hips so she faced him. "I could have sat the other way, but I want your mouth on my nipples."

Brandon gave her a dramatic sigh, so unlike him that she snorted. "If you really want me to, I guess I can suck your nipples. But I'll have to bite them, too." He gave her a serious look.

God, she could fall in love with this man.

She nodded. "If biting is what you need, I suppose that will work."

Avery was still laughing as he impaled her with his cock. The laugh ended on a strangled moan, and the two of them rocked their hips together, his length stretching her in just the right way.

He palmed her ass as she rode him, pressing her chest to his face so he could do as he'd promised and take care of her breasts. And as she came, he hammered into her harder before pulling her off of him. Her body was languid, and yet it heated all over again at the sight of him naked, sweaty, and hard. She let him move her around to find the best position. The couch was just wide enough to make this work, and for that, she was grateful. She wasn't sure she'd have lasted long enough for the time it would have taken to get back to the bedroom.

He had her back to his front, and her legs pressed tightly together. Then he entered her slowly, the position making her feel as if he were getting larger and longer within her. She twisted back so she could kiss him as he placed one hand on her hip, keeping her steady as he fucked her. The other hand he rested on her breast and then slid up to her neck.

And when they came, they kissed each other, swallowing each other's moans, and she knew that no matter how long she lived, she would never tire of this man.

And, it was only the beginning.

CHAPTER 13

THE DREAM STARTED out the same as last time, and Brandon knew he'd have to go with it or end up in pain from fighting it again. He screamed as teeth bit into his flesh, the eyes of the wolf at his side sorrowful yet full of a rage that wasn't quite kept in check.

Brandon fell to the ground at his brothers' sides. He didn't want to die this way but had a feeling this was the end. This wolf had won, and Brandon hadn't been strong enough to fight.

The dream faded but not fully. This time, a woman with long, dark hair and bright blue eyes stared at him, her long, flowing, white dress waving in a breeze he couldn't feel.

"You're not dying, Brandon," she said softly.

He *knew* that voice; had heard it on the wind in his childhood and later when he'd become the Omega.

"Goddess?"

She smiled softly at him, and he knew this was no mere dream. This was something else, and there was no way he was hallucinating or making this up. He wasn't sure he had the imagination to come up with anything like this.

"You're not dying, Brandon," she repeated. There was just something so otherworldly about her that he knew this had to be the moon goddess. He had countless questions, and yet nothing to say. What could he say in her presence? What could he ask?

"You're such an old soul, my Brandon. Much like your brothers, Kameron and Walker. The three of you were born under the same moon and have always been as one. You were once man, then wolf, now man and wolf. You have lived before, your soul not young, but aged and worn."

Brandon sat up within his dream, his body not aching at all despite the fact that he'd almost died a few moments ago. The wolf stood frozen at his side, agony within its eyes. His brothers lay to the right, frozen in time, as well.

He thought over her words and frowned. "Are you saying...this was a past life that I'm seeing?"

She smiled. "You were always so clever, Brandon. The

first brother to find his mates, the first brother to do so in the past, as well." She waved at the wolf at Brandon's side. "This was my first wolf." Sadness crossed her face. "I have always regretted the pain I caused him—the pain I caused his line. Yes, he broke our laws, but he never deserved the agony he suffered." She looked directly at Brandon, a fierceness in her eyes he couldn't comprehend. "I couldn't take away the wolf or the way one must become another, but I gave him his bonds to a Pack he formed on his own. I gave him the ability to love so deeply that eons of time wouldn't be enough for a mating bond to break. You are of the first wolves to be made—you and your brothers." She looked away as Brandon's entire being rocked at her words.

"Are you saying I'm of that line?" Or was it something more.

"You are both," she answered, not looking at him. "You are of that lineage, yes, but you are something more, as well. You were *him*."

Brandon blinked. "Are you talking about reincarnation?" One day, he would sit down with the rest of his family and tell them about this conversation with a goddess about wolves and reincarnation, but he was pretty sure either way he'd feel off-kilter.

She nodded, still not looking at him. "That is one word for it." She looked at him again. "I grow old, young one. As do my people. The world has changed so much in such a short time, and I'm afraid of what might come next."

Chills racked his body. If a goddess was afraid…then perhaps there truly was no hope for them.

"What can we do?" he asked, his voice breaking.

"There is one…" She trailed off. "There is a chance. Beyond the lines and divisions, there is one who can save you, save us. One that will need your help.

"*A wolf of three Packs can break their will or unite them all.*

"*Once united, the Packs will reveal…*

"*If broken, the Packs will fall…*"

Her mouth didn't move as the last three sentences were whispered in his ear. He blinked, trying to understand what had just happened. But before he could ask, he opened his eyes and found himself once again in his bed, Avery wrapped around his side and Parker tucked in safely behind her.

Holy shit.

He sat up, carefully untangling himself from Avery so he wouldn't wake her or Parker. He let the goddess's words roll around in his brain as he tried to make sense of them. But the thing was, he'd heard those words before—from *Parker*. It was the same prophecy the European elders had told him when Parker had touched the spear.

Between that and the moon goddess, whatever those words meant, it was important. He looked over at his mates' sleeping forms, a frown on his face. The last two sentences of the prophecy seemed to be the outcome of the first. Meaning it was *who* the prophecy was about that was important.

And there was only one person Brandon knew that carried the blood of three Packs within his veins.

And he was sleeping in Brandon's bed.

Before Brandon could let that settle over him, the house shook as an explosion rang out. He was out of bed and had his feet stuffed into his boots in the next instant. Parker had done the same thing next to him, while Avery scrambled out of bed, sliding into the jeans they'd left on the floor the night before.

"What's going on?" she asked, her voice alert for this time of night.

Brandon's phone buzzed on the nightstand, and he answered it quickly. "What is it?"

"Bombing outside the north gate," Mitchell answered, his voice a growl. "You and Parker get out here now and be ready to fight. There's a group of men and women in all black with guns and other weapons, ready to take us down." He paused. "Send Avery to the infirmary with Leah. She's not ready to fight yet, but she can help there."

Brandon bit out a curse. "Got it." He tucked his phone

in his pocket and slid on a shirt. He'd have to fight in sweats, but that was fine since he might have to shift later anyway.

"We heard," Avery said as she tied her shoes. "Wolf hearing is something I'm going to have to get used to." She spoke so quickly, he knew she was trying to hold back her panic. This wasn't the world she'd grown up in, and hell, it wasn't quite the life he'd had either, but she was still moving forward as best she could.

Parker kissed her hard, and then Brandon moved closer to do the same.

"Be safe," Brandon said softly.

Avery looked between them, her eyes gold. "You two are the ones going out there, so you both had better be safe." She gripped their hands. "Take care of one another, okay?"

Brandon squeezed her hand and nodded before pulling away and heading out of the house, Parker by his side. Avery jogged the other direction, and people moved quickly around them, going to their posts. The maternals and submissives would protect the children, while the dominants would secure the perimeter and fight. If anyone somehow got through the wards, the adult wolves inside would fight to the death for the children, regardless of their wolf's dominance. It was how their Pack worked—at least now. It hadn't been that way under the old Alpha

—his father's regime—and that was one thing Brandon was happy about.

Parker and Brandon hurried to the north gate in silence, no words needing to be said. He firmly pushed all thoughts of prophecies and reincarnation out of his mind, his wolf ready to take down anyone that threatened his den. They were at Mitchell's and Kameron's sides quickly, each of their wolves ready.

"What do we have?" Brandon asked. This wasn't Parker's Pack, and though things might change soon, it was Brandon who needed to ask the questions.

"Bombing knocked down a few trees and fucked with some of our surveillance, but no one was hurt," Kameron said. "Only problem is that there's a group out there dressed like fucking commandos, and they're way too organized to be a simple hate group."

"Shit," Parker growled.

"Shit is right," Mitchell spat. "We're waiting on the go-ahead from Gideon, but we'll have to take them out. Either by knocking them unconscious or literally if they're a true threat. We already staked our claim on this land in front of the world, and rolling back now will do us no good."

Brandon nodded, agreeing. When Gideon let out a howl, he growled, moving forward with the rest of them. The die had been cast, and now it was time to protect their den—even if it left a mark on their souls in the process.

As soon as they'd slid through the wards, the unit in front of them moved, guns firing before anyone had a chance to take a breath. Brandon ducked out of the way, his wolf at the surface so his reflexes were faster than normal. He took down the closest attacker, knocking him out so he'd be down for the count for a few hours at least. Parker fought at his side, doing the same to the human near him. They didn't want to kill anyone, but damn it, these guys were firing at them, and Brandon knew blood would spill that night.

The group might be highly organized and much more than a simple hate-crime group, but the wolves were better, faster. Each of his Packmates took down the enemy one by one, not having to take a single life. He *knew* this was too easy, and felt that there was something wrong, but he couldn't stop to think about it or he'd end up dead.

As soon as they'd gotten the last one down and began tying them up, a *click* sounded in Brandon's ear, and he turned. Mitchell threw Parker to the ground next to them, and time froze.

His cousin roared, blood gushing from his leg as he rolled off Parker and slammed his hand over the wound. A clearly shaken Parker snarled before leaping up higher than Brandon thought possible into the tree closest to them. Moments later, a man with a rifle fell out of the tree, neck broken and his body lying in a heap like a ragdoll. Parker jumped out of the tree at that instant, his gaze gold, and his chest heaving.

Brandon let out a breath, kneeling at Mitchell's side and trying to stop the blood flow.

"Hit my fucking artery," Mitchell gritted out. "Fucking coward, doing that after everything else was clear and he thought he was safe."

Parker growled low next to them. "Would have killed me," he said, his voice all wolf, no trace of man.

"But it didn't," Walker put in. "Now get out of my way so I can heal him. Mitchell, you're going to have to shift, and it's going to hurt like a motherfucker, but it's the only way I'm going to be able to stop the bleeding out here."

Mitchell paled but did as he was told. Brandon helped Parker strip Mitchell out of his clothes as the others worked to form a protective circle around them. It would be too dangerous to move behind the wards, but no one dared say that.

Brandon saw the guilt in Parker's eyes and knew he'd have to do something about it soon, but first, he needed to make sure his cousin was safe. Mitchell didn't make a sound through most of his shifting while Walker clamped his hand over the wound. Having to shift with someone holding you and while you were in pain had to be excruciating, but it wasn't until the end when Walker had his hand on Mitchell's fur that his cousin let out a small whine. That enraged Brandon's wolf, and he let out a tiny growl, pissed off that people were *still* trying to kill his family just because they weren't *normal*.

Finally, Walker wavered, his body weakening from the amount of power he must have had to use on Mitchell, and Parker went to help the other man stand. "Let's get back inside," Walker said when he was on his feet.

"I'll stay behind to help clean up the mess," Parker said, his voice devoid of emotion.

Kameron shot Brandon a look, but Brandon shook his head. If Parker needed to do something to get over his guilt, then, for now, he would let him. When they were alone with Avery or even alone together later, he'd figure out the best way to make sure his mate understood that this wasn't this fault.

The blame belonged to those who wanted to hurt them. Those that didn't understand them. And each attack was getting more organized and hurting them more and more. There was only so much they could take until one day they broke.

The prophecy came to his mind again, and Brandon froze. It meant something...but what? What could they do when the world seemed bleak and there were no obvious answers?

Brandon wasn't sure, but no matter what, he wouldn't let those he cared about drown alone.

Not again.

CHAPTER 14

"AVERY'S STILL AT THE INFIRMARY?" Parker asked as he sat down to take off his boots.

"Yeah, Leah is helping her get to know the area since she felt like she couldn't do much," Brandon answered. The other man sat on the coffee table across from Parker, a frown on his face, but hadn't said much since Parker had come back home from cleaning up after the attack.

"Mitchell doing okay?" He did his best to keep his emotions out of his words, but since the man was the damn Omega, Brandon didn't fall for it.

"He'll be fine. And what happened wasn't your fault."

Parker shook his head. "I don't want to get into it."

"Well, tough shit. I don't really give a damn what you want right now. I'm going to give you what you need."

Parker's head shot up as heat went straight to his

groin. "That sounds like you want to bend me over and fuck me."

Brandon growled again and pinched Parker's chin. "I just might, but first, you're going to listen to me. You are *not* at fault for what happened tonight. That loser with the gun is—was."

"But if I hadn't been so much slower than usual, I wouldn't have needed Mitchell to throw me out of the way."

Brandon snarled. "You don't know that. You honestly don't know that, and Mitchell was the one that risked himself. He did it because that's the kind of man he is. He could have yelled at you. Hell, *I* could have yelled to you, but Mitchell was faster than that. He has a death wish. He puts his life on the line every damn time he can. I don't fucking know why, but I'm going to find out. What happened tonight was not your fault."

Parker closed his eyes, trying to get the sight of Mitchell's blood pooling around him out of his mind. "I still feel like shit."

Brandon sighed. "Well, yeah. You have a curse on your body that can apparently only be fixed by mating, and since none of us are there yet, you're weakening."

He opened his eyes, frowning. "I don't want us to go into eternity together only because we want to save each other's lives. We all deserve better than that."

Brandon moved forward and rested his hands on Parker's thighs. Parker's cock filled, pressing against his pants. And since he wore sweats, he made a nice tent. He looked down at Brandon's waist and held back a grin. It seemed Brandon had also pitched a pretty nice tent.

"We're going to have better than that. We have time." The other man let out a breath, his hands rubbing Parker's thighs.

"If you're going to rub me, you might as well make it worth it," Parker teased.

Brandon's grip tightened. "Tease."

Parker lifted his butt to pull down his sweats. Since he hadn't bothered to put on underwear, his cock sprang free, as hard as a pipe. "Not teasing. I want your mouth on me."

Brandon raised a brow. "I'll suck you down, but that means I get to fuck your face later."

Parker snorted. "A negotiation?"

Brandon reached forward and squeezed the base of Parker's cock. Hard. Parker's eyes crossed, and he gasped for breath.

"Negotiate all you want," he croaked.

"I think I will," Brandon said before he leaned down and swallowed him whole.

Parker *loved* blowjobs. He loved eating pussy, as well. There was nothing as intimate as someone you cared about—someone you were falling in love with—with their head between your legs and vice versa. And while Parker felt he was talented at giving blowjobs, he had *nothing* on Brandon.

Holy. Hell.

Brandon hollowed his cheeks, using his tongue and suction to make Parker almost blow his load too soon. Then the other man scraped his hands down Parker's thighs, and once again, Parker almost lost it.

Not wanting to end too quickly, he tugged Brandon up and took his mouth with his. The other man's lips were wet and swollen, and he could taste himself on his tongue.

Brandon was still jerking Parker off as they made out on the couch, so Parker slid his hand under the edge of Brandon's sweats and squeezed the other man's length. Soon, both of them had their pants off and were lying face to face on the couch, kissing and sucking on each other's mouths and necks, all the while, jerking each other off while thrusting so they rubbed against each other, as well. He hadn't made out like this since he was a teenager and had found a human boy who liked it rough.

Now, he was a man with healthier appetites and had a fucking sexy male in his arms.

"I need you," Parker gasped as Brandon did this twisting move with his hand that made Parker's eyes cross.

"No room here," Brandon bit out. "We're both too big."

"Yeah, we are," Parker teased.

Brandon rolled his eyes. "Yeah, you've got a big cock. Me, too. Let's play with them some more in bed where I can spread you out."

A sensual shiver slid down Parker's spine, and he stood up with Brandon, following him to the bedroom. Usually, Brandon was the calmer of the two of them, less likely to make a joke or laugh. Yet, apparently, as soon as Brandon got naked and his cock got hard, the man had a sense of humor.

Between Brandon and Avery, Parker was one lucky man.

The two of them stood at the end of the bed after Brandon had pulled out the lube from the bedside table. They were still kissing, running their hands all over one another as if they couldn't stop.

"Are you going to fuck me this time?" Brandon asked, need in his voice.

Parker leaned forward and bit Brandon's lip. "As long as you fuck me next time."

"Deal."

They kissed some more, their bodies heating as their hands slid over one another, and they readied each other for what was to come. Eventually, Brandon lay on his back, his fist pumping slowly over his cock as Parker spread the other man's legs.

"Let me know if I hurt you."

Brandon raised a brow. "Thinking mighty big of yourself there."

Parker narrowed his eyes and thrust slightly, pushing the head of his cock past Brandon's ring of muscle.

"Shit. Okay, fuck, yeah, you're big."

Parker froze. "Am I hurting you?" He licked his lips, sweat beading on his forehead.

"No, just surprised me. Keep going. You slicked me up already, Parker. You're not going to hurt me."

Parker ran his hands down Brandon's thighs before holding onto the other man's hips. "Okay, then." Then he pushed in a little bit more. Then a little bit more. Then, *finally*, they both moved as one, their bodies sweaty, their mouths meeting, and Brandon's cock between them.

Parker would never forget the glassy-eyed look that swept across Brandon's face as he came. Parker followed him, the bond between them flaring once more as it tried to settle into place. But without the mating mark, it wouldn't stay. They kissed a few more moments before Parker pulled out and went to get a washcloth to clean them both. Soon, they were holding one another, aware that Avery would be home soon and would be able to join them in their pile of limbs and heat.

As they fell asleep, tangled as one, Parker didn't think about the near miss and what had happened earlier.

Instead, he dreamt of the two people in the world who could make him see life for what it was and what it needed to be.

And he didn't worry what would happen if they never bonded...because if he thought about that, then he might never sleep again.

CHAPTER 15

AVERY PRESSED the shutter down once more, knowing that the shot in the end would be exactly what she wanted. She lowered her arms, her camera in her hands and a sense of peace washing over her for the first time in what felt like weeks.

She was a photojournalist, or at least, that's who she had been. That's what she'd made herself so she could *do* something in a world where she felt helpless and in need of a life where she was something more. Some of the wolves outside the den had cleared her old apartment for her safety, and now she had her camera and everything she needed for work—not that things would ever go back to the way they once were.

She let out a sigh and turned away from the building she'd taken a photo of. She wouldn't take pictures of her new Packmates unless she had their permission, but there were sites in the den she knew she needed to capture. While many were tense about what was going on around them, there were still key slices of life happening that proved, no matter what, people *lived*.

And that is what I do, I record that, Avery thought with a sigh. Or rather, it's what she had done. She glimpsed life at it's weakest, at it's fullest, and everything in between and did her best to take a snapshot of what she could, to freeze that point in time so others could know that these few lived.

That they thrived.

Avery looked down at her camera, a frown on her face. She didn't know what she would do next, how her life would change yet again with each passing breath, but she prayed she could at least keep this.

Because *this* was something she could do for her new family.

At least, she hoped so.

Avery's back hit the ground, and she gasped for breath. She rolled over to get back on her feet but she wasn't quite fast enough. Kameron reached out and gripped her ankle, tugging her back to the ground.

She snarled, her wolf pissed off that she wasn't getting this, and slammed her hand on the ground twice.

"I yield."

Kameron let go but held out his hand to help her up. "You're not as bad as you think you are."

Avery rubbed her nose with her middle finger at that remark, and Kameron grinned. She was so taken aback by the fact that this man actually *smiled*, that she almost tripped over her feet. While she knew Brandon, Walker, and Kameron were triplets, they were almost nothing alike. Brandon cut himself off from emotion unless he was with just Avery and Parker, and even that wasn't that often. Walker seemed the most approachable of the three, but she had a feeling that was just a facade to hide what he was really feeling. Kameron, on the other hand, never hid his emotions. The only problem there was that the emotions he showed were icy-cold and full of rage. She had no idea what had happened to him in the past, but she had a feeling whatever man or woman eventually found a way through that frigid shell to mate with him was going to have a tough road ahead of them.

Of course, it wasn't like her path was easy. Hell, it had been nothing *but* bumps, and she knew the time for holding back was coming to a close. Her men were hurting, and her wolf *begged* her daily for the two of them. She just had to take the leap of faith of a lifetime and pray she wasn't making a huge mistake. She'd leapt once already for them and hadn't crashed and burned. Maybe fully creating the bond would finally let her wolf—and world—settle down a fraction.

"You're lost in your mind again, little girl. That's going to get you in trouble one of these days."

She narrowed her eyes at Kameron. "First, I'm a woman. Not a little girl."

"You're far younger than I am."

She rolled her eyes. "Honey, I'm with Brandon, your triplet. You saying things like that just makes it weird. So don't. And secondly, you don't know a thing about me, so why don't you lay off. Oh, and thirdly? My mind gets me in all sorts of trouble but, hell, it's also what gets me out of it. As you can see, fighting hasn't really been helping." She held out her hands and gave him a self-deprecating smile.

Kameron snorted, and Avery took that as a win. "Jesus, between you and Parker, my baby brother has his hands full."

She flipped him off again. "You're a triplet. He can't be your baby brother."

"I disagree. I'm the eldest triplet, thank you very much."

Avery laughed, shaking her head. "Okay, I guess that counts. Just a little bit, though."

"I'm glad I have your approval," he said dryly. "As for

what you said before, you're right, I *don't* know you. I don't know anything about you except for who your father is." He held up his hand when she opened her mouth. "If you'd known our father, you would have run away from us if you thought we were anything like him. Hell, the whole generation before us was a group of sadistic assholes that liked torturing people for fun. Sounds like your pops. But, Avery? You're not him. I get that, but you're also getting closer and closer to my brother. So, yeah, I'm going to watch out for him by watching you. Call me an asshole all you want, but I'm still going to be an asshole once you see why I'm doing it. I'm *always* an asshole."

She blinked at his words. Not just what he'd said, but the amount of them. Kameron wasn't much for talking, and yet he'd said so much right then.

"Brandon said some things about your father, but not much," she said finally after a moment. She held up her hands right after she said it. "But when he's ready, he'll tell me the rest. I won't ask that of you."

Kameron's eyes flared gold. "Maybe you'll be good for him yet."

She flipped him off again before crouching down into position. "Again?"

Kameron nodded. "The humans who are coming at the den are much slower than you, and you're slower than the rest of us, so that's saying something."

"I'd flip you off again but it's getting tedious," she said dryly.

"What I'm saying is that you have to listen to your wolf, even though it's a new thing, and learn to use that newfound speed."

"But they're using guns and other weapons. I can't use my claws in human form."

Kameron nodded. "That's why you're also taking weapons training. We all carry weapons—and not just our claws. We try not to use them because while we're protecting our den, we can't kill *everyone* that threatens us." He snarled. "Though I'm tempted to take out the lot of them, it would only harm us in the long run. We're trying to remain citizens and *human* in the eyes of the law."

"And killing even in self-defense is a mark against you." She thought of how Parker had killed the man in the tree but felt no remorse. That soldier—or whoever he'd been—had almost killed Mitchell and Parker. And if he hadn't been taken out when he was, he could have hurt so many others. The Talons had been forced into fighting with one hand tied behind their backs, and it was no wonder they felt as if they were on the losing end of a war that refused to be out in the open with clear and defined rules.

Kameron's jaw tightened. "Exactly. Now go!"

. . .

After another hour of getting her ass handed to her by Kameron, Avery's bones ached, and she was pretty sure her muscles would never be the same. Between training during the days and nights with her men, her body hurt. Kameron finally let her go after she'd failed to take out his legs for what felt like the eight-hundredth time. Now, she lay facedown on the couch, her face buried in a throw pillow, willing her body to move so she could get up and get some cake. Not that they had cake in the house since she lived with boys and they didn't think to have cake for emergencies like this, but maybe there would be something sweet to eat to make her feel better.

If she hadn't already spent her life running from the evil that was her father and using her lens to capture the war-torn areas of the world, she might have worried at how quickly she'd adjusted to living with a Pack of shifters and sleeping between *two* of them every night. Yet when she tried to see if she would panic about it, she couldn't. It just *was*. There was no use freaking out over the fact that her life had changed so completely when a small part of her had always known she'd become a wolf. She'd go insane if she did. She'd seen it in her visions, after all—even if she didn't truly understand it until much later.

Avery had never been one to dwell on what she didn't have because she'd never been able to hold onto things for long.

Maybe that's why she'd been holding back from Parker and Brandon as she had. At that disturbing thought, she rolled over and forced herself to sit up. The men would be coming home soon, and she needed to get her head on straight. For one, she kept calling Brandon's place *home,* and she liked the fact that she did. She knew that no matter what happened next, she wanted to stay here with Brandon *and* Parker. They were *hers.* Yes, it scared her in some ways, but in others, she honestly couldn't wait for them to be whole without this looming decision over their heads.

Two very sexy male scents hit her senses right before the front door opened. That was one thing she found super weird about this whole new wolf thing. She could *hear* and *scent* people before they came into her view, and that was saying something considering she could see better, as well. It would all be overwhelming if Brandon and Parker weren't teaching her how to control that aspect of her new life. Her two men were truly running themselves ragged trying to help her, as they tried to stay healthy, save the Pack, and go about their normal duties, as well.

Brandon's face broke out into a smile as soon as he saw

her, the tired lines on his face smoothing out. Parker smiled, as well, though he couldn't hide the dark circles under his eyes at all.

They were dying because of forces out of their control, and she'd been forced to hold back from mating with them not only because of insecurities but also the fact that it could hurt *her*.

She'd gladly take the pain if she could wipe away theirs.

And it was time to do something about that.

"We ran into Kameron on our way back," Parker said as he took a seat on the end of the couch. He lifted her feet into his lap and began rubbing. She'd have been embarrassed by the moan coming out of her mouth if she hadn't moaned like crazy already for them before. Often.

"He said you're doing better," Brandon added. He sat behind her and began rubbing her shoulders.

Avery closed her eyes and let her men take care of her, their hands strong and a little rough—just the way she liked it. She'd either come or fall asleep if they kept touching her, and honestly, that sounded like the best night ever. But first, she wanted to tell them exactly why she was the way she was...and maybe take the next step that they'd all been avoiding for her safety. Too much change and too much power in so little time could kill her —at least that's what they'd worried about.

It was time for Avery to take care of her men.

"My visions weren't always so frequent," she began. Both men froze for a bare instant before going back to rubbing her feet and back. "When I was a child, I didn't even realize they *were* visions. I just thought they were weird dreams. I didn't realize they sometimes came true until I was older." She let out a breath, remembering the time she'd seen her teacher have a heart attack on the playground the day before it had happened.

"I cried on my mom's lap when I told her about my teacher," she continued. "She held me and comforted me before telling me to *never* tell anyone but her what I'd seen." Parker reached forward and cupped her cheek, rubbing away her tears. Brandon pressed a soft kiss to the back of her neck, and she felt like she had the strength to continue. "I didn't know she'd meant my father when she said that."

Her voice broke, and both men held her. She straightened between them, needing to get the rest out. "My mother saw the future, too. She'd kept it hidden from my father because she knew he wouldn't have understood. I don't know why she married him, nor do I know why they stayed together. But that's…that's not what I want to get into right now."

She paused a moment to collect her thoughts.

"I had another vision one afternoon when my mom

was at the grocery store. My father was actually home instead of on base dealing with his job. He was usually there instead of home, which I never put too much thought into. I thought all fathers slept over at the base most nights. I thought all fathers cared about their men more than their family. But I was so scared about the vision I'd had of blood on my mother's face that I went straight to him." She let out a shaky breath. "I told him what I had seen, and he asked all these probing questions that I was too young to understand. Too young to know I needed to lie. So in the end, I told him I could see the future, and so could my mother."

"Oh, baby," Parker whispered. He ran his hand up her leg and leaned closer. Brandon stayed silent but his touches never stopped. They both knew what kind of monster her father had been, so what she said next wasn't as shocking as it probably should have been.

"I never saw my mom again. The morning she left with a kiss on my temple, and a grocery list in her hand, was the last time I saw her alive. Dad had her taken to one of his labs." She spat out the words. "I only know what he did to her because he told me later. Showed me the photos when I wouldn't obey him or tell him what he needed to know about his enemies. My visions never came on command, and they never will, but he didn't understand that. He *tortured* his wife, my mother, to see how she worked. And when her body couldn't take it anymore, he killed her."

Both men held her as she cried, her body shaking.

"When he told me the truth of it, that she hadn't been hit by a car on her way home from the grocery store like he'd first told me, I ran." She pressed her lips together. "I ran as far as I could and lived on the street until I found a nice family who helped me grow up enough to live on my own. I didn't live under the name Montag and changed my name constantly, but eventually, Dad quit looking for me. And when I started to make a name for myself in photojournalism, he still didn't come after me. I don't know why, maybe because he had his sights set on the wolves and not whatever he thought I was, but I stayed away from him, too. I stayed away from anything having to do with him until I saw what he'd done, watched it happen on-screen." She wiped away her tears, leaning on her men. "And that's why I came here, why I *am* here. I ran for so long. I don't want to run anymore."

She shifted so she sat on the edge of the couch and was able to turn and face each of them when needed. Only Brandon's arm on her back and Parker's on her leg kept her from falling off the couch. And yet, she trusted them to never let her fall, never let go.

And that's why she was going to give in...finally.

"I don't want to wait anymore," she whispered. "I'm

falling for both of you, and I want to take the next step. I don't want to go into the next weeks not having both of you connected to me on a fundamental level. I know you're worried about how a new bond will affect my wolf, but we've waited long enough." She raised her chin, her heart in her throat. "My wolf is strong—stronger than she was when we first found out that we might be mates. I *know* we're mates...we just need to let ourselves fall."

Brandon cupped her face. "I don't want you to mate with us because you feel like you need to save us."

Anger rushed into her. "So what if I want to save you? So the fuck what? I want you in my life, Brandon. I want Parker in my life. And that's not going to happen if you fade away because you need a mating bond and don't have one. *I'm right here.* I don't want to mate with you to save you, I want to mate with you because I'm falling in love with you. And if saving your life is a byproduct of that, then, damn it, I *need* the bond."

Parker wrapped his hand around her hair and tugged her face to his. He didn't kiss her, instead he looked right into her eyes. "I won't ask if you're sure because I don't want to tell you what to think, but Avery? I'm not falling in love with you." A shocking pain sliced through her. "I'm already *in* love with you. Both of you."

She punched him in the chest. "That was a horrible way to say that."

Parker winced, rubbing his chest. "I'm not the eloquent one in this relationship."

They both looked to Brandon, who raised a brow. "And you think *I'm* the eloquent one?" He shook his head. "I'd already fallen for the idea of both of you before I even met you, yet the real thing? The real thing is so much more intense than I ever thought possible. I want that future together, whatever it may hold in the coming days. You're each a rock that holds me in place, that keeps me from faltering. Of course, I love you both."

Tears in her eyes, she met Parker's gaze. "And he says he's not the eloquent one."

Parker laughed softly before leaning forward. "Mine."

Then he kissed her, almost sending Avery over the edge from a bare meeting of lips alone.

They'd all been together so many times before that she knew this time wouldn't be slow. No, they needed each other, needed this bond *now*. Later, they would go back and hold each other, kiss and lick every inch of each other, but for now, they just needed to be inside one another.

When they were all naked and Brandon entered her, she arched into him, her wolf ready for what came next. She met her mate's eyes, knowing that this was a moment that would be seared into her memory for all eternity. Her fangs elongated at the same time as his, and she instinctively knew where to bite, where to *mark*. She bit into his shoulder, marking him as hers. And just like that, the mating bond snapped into place. She threw her head back and screamed, her body shaking as she came, Brandon's emotions and feelings slamming into her all at once, as if she were living one moment amongst many, their lives forever entangled.

There wasn't enough time to fully process what had happened before Parker was over her, making sweet love to her as Brandon filled Parker from behind. They marked each other, as well, her wolf howling at the unseen moon as the three of them found their bonds.

Three wolves. Three people. One mating.

They were hers.

Her men.

Her future.

Her mates.

And nothing had ever felt like this…and she knew, nothing ever would. This hadn't been too soon, hadn't been a mistake. This had been her destiny. She'd only had to find it.

CHAPTER 16

BRANDON RUBBED HIS CHEST, the mating mark pulsating as he thought of the two individuals by his side. He was *mated*. He wasn't sure how he'd ended up so lucky, to have mated with the two people who made him whole, but he knew he would never take them for granted.

Now, he sat in Gideon's home, Avery tucked close to him with Parker on her other side, as his family came together to discuss what their future plans were, as well as what had happened over the past few weeks.

So much had changed, and yet, what was to come hadn't.

Gideon and Brie huddled together, while Brynn and Finn—though Redwoods now, were still family—sat beside them on another loveseat. Charlotte, Shane, and Bram might not be Brentwoods either, but they had been adopted into the family nonetheless and had been invited to this meeting. Ryder had Leah on his lap, the witch on the verge of a nap. Brandon had a feeling the couple was either trying to have a child or would soon announce a pregnancy. Mitchell and Max sat on the floor as always, the brothers close no matter the room they settled in. Kameron and Walker were on the couch nearest Brandon and his mates, in deep conversation about something Brandon had a feeling they would let him in on soon. They were triplets, after all.

"The government is still trying to decide what to do with us." Gideon rubbed the back of his neck with one hand, his arm around a *very* pregnant Brie with the other. She was almost a full week past due, and the Alpha's nerves were shot. "Either they'll decide we're human enough to be granted full rights and then we'll have the law behind us as we continue to try and survive, or we'll lose and have to fight even harder."

"But no matter what the law says, there will still be some that threaten us because we're different," Brandon said softly, though his voice held more strength than it had in months.

"I have a feeling the President will stand by our side," Kameron said after a moment. He looked up when the room went silent. "He's not the final voice if Congress makes a move, but he's the loudest."

"It's an election year, and McMaster is vying for the President's seat," Mitchell put in.

"And he'll lose," Avery said suddenly. "Because he has to. Evil cannot win."

Brandon squeezed her shoulder and let out a breath. "We can hope."

"I don't like this kind of fighting," Max said after they'd discussed their plans for the patrols and government issues. "It's easier to fight with your fists than stand back and let people who don't understand what they're talking about try to use big words to tell us we aren't human."

Brandon reached out and gripped Max's shoulder since his cousin was so close. "We'll figure it out."

"We always do," Parker whispered.

And Brandon hoped what they said was true.

Gideon cleared his throat. "I called this family meeting to not only talk about certain logistics but to welcome two new members to the Pack *and* our family." Gideon grinned and Brandon practically puffed out his chest.

Yeah, he had *two* mates with him on the couch. Count 'em. Two. Eventually, his wolf would stop acting so cocky, but it was so damned happy to finally have mating bonds to roll around in.

Avery blushed and turned her head into him, hiding

her face. She might be the toughest woman he'd ever met in his long life, but she hated being the center of attention.

"Parker, Avery, welcome to our Pack," Gideon said, his voice that of the Alpha. "And welcome to our family as mates of Brandon." This time, his voice was that of a brother, family. Gideon had become adept at finding a balance between the two over the years, but it had been his mating with Brie, a submissive wolf from the Redwood Pack, that had made him who he was today. A man Brandon was truly honored to call Alpha.

"Thank you," Parker said with a soft growl. His wolf was in his voice, and Brandon knew that was because he was trying to come to terms with not only a new Pack but also a new Alpha. Parker's wolf was freaking *strong*—far stronger now that he was whole and healthy from the mating bonds. Brandon had a feeling if his mate ever wanted to be an Alpha, the moon goddess would grant him that blessing—and burden. Yet because Avery and Brandon had both been Talons, *and* Brandon was the Omega—a position he couldn't relinquish—Parker had chosen to break his bond with the Redwoods and his family and become a Talon, as well. Though both Packs were so entwined now, the break wouldn't be as bad as it had been even a few short years ago.

"I know you're the Voice of the Wolves and will

continue to be so," Gideon said, "but I'd like to make you a Lieutenant within the Pack, as well."

Brandon grinned. "That's a wolf who protects the Alpha and the Pack," he said to Avery.

She nodded. "I know. I've been learning." Of course, she was. She may have been forced to jump into this life blindly, but he knew she wouldn't stay that way if given a choice.

Parker nodded solemnly. "I'd be honored."

Gideon smiled. "Good. We can do the full ceremony later once you've had time to let the new Pack and mating bonds settle." He turned to Avery. "With the strength of your wolf, I had thought you would be good as a sentry, soldier, or even a Lieutenant, but I'm not going to put you as any of those."

Brandon frowned, and Parker let out a small growl. The others started talking, and Gideon held up his hand.

"Wait, let me explain. It was Brie who finally made me understand that I would have been wrong to assign you any of those duties." He stood up, leaving Brie alone on the loveseat, telling Brandon that whatever Gideon had to say was important. There was no way the other man would freely leave his pregnant mate's side in any other circumstance. He knelt before Avery—something an Alpha rarely if *ever* did—and a few of Brandon's family members gasped. "You're a dominant wolf, Avery, but that's not all. And if you think hard, I bet you know what you are."

She licked her lips. "I...I don't know if I'm right."

"You are, Avery. Tell me what group I should place you in to protect and honor our Pack."

She lowered her gaze, her voice soft when she finally spoke, "I'm a maternal dominant."

Brandon's wolf howled, everything finally clicking into place. The way Avery worked with her wolf finally made sense. She fought with all her heart but also needed to care for those around her. Maternal dominants protected the young of the Pack but also fought alongside the soldiers in other cases.

Maternal dominants were rare, but he knew his Avery would do her new title justice.

Gideon cupped her face, and Brandon didn't feel a lick of jealousy. This was his Alpha protecting his people, not a man and a woman. "You will do us proud, Avery. Always."

The others stood, and the entire Brentwood clan welcomed Avery and Parker into their fold. Brandon had never felt more like a true Talon Pack member than he did right then, and that's why he had to tell them of his dreams.

He'd already told Parker and Avery about them, but he hadn't told them of the visit from the moon goddess.

For some reason, he'd *known* he needed to wait until he was with Kameron and Walker to tell them what he'd seen.

And since Parker had already told him that he was going to talk about the prophecy during the meeting, right now seemed like the right time to share.

Once everyone had settled down, he cleared his throat. "I have something to say, if you don't mind."

Everyone looked at him, and he didn't fault them their curious gazes. Brandon didn't normally speak at these functions, the emotions within the room usually so intense he could barely hold onto the stream of conversation, let alone join in. But now that he had two other people sharing his burden—without feeling the side effects—he could finally breathe again. He truly understood now why Omegas *always* had mates.

Avery squeezed his hand, and Parker reached over to brush against his shoulder, with their strength, he could do this.

"I've been having dreams," he began. It was a testament to what they'd all gone through over the past few years with Gideon, Ryder, Brynn, and so on, that no one laughed at his odd announcement.

"What kind of dreams?" Walker asked, a frown on his face.

"Ones that felt like they were slowly sucking the life

out of me because I couldn't understand them. They felt like memories, yet what happened in them had never happened to me. At least not the me you see here."

Kameron's brows rose. "You're going to have to be a little more clear. Not all of us have the same brain capacity as Walker over there." He gestured to his brother.

Brandon's mouth ticked up in a small smile, grateful his siblings helped him with the tension so he could collect his thoughts. "They *were* memories. Ones that came from a lifetime of lifetimes ago, a life I lived but had forgotten."

Brynn's eyes widened. "You're talking about reincarnation. That's actually a thing?"

Brandon snorted as the others turned to him, wide eyes on each of them. "Yes, it's apparently a thing. The moon goddess told me so." He shook his head as the others started asking him question after question. "I'm getting ahead of myself, and I need to start at the beginning. The dreams were painful, but not just because I was reliving what happened. It's about *what* happened in the dreams. You see, the first hunter, the first wolf, bit me. And I became one of the three first wolves made from a bite." He looked over at Kameron and Walker who had gone still. "My brothers, you two, were the other two men who were made wolves. All three of us were once a part of the original Pack. We're old souls, reborn. What that means? I don't know exactly, but it's *important*."

"Holy shit," Avery whispered and some in the room laughed, the tension easing fractionally. "Sorry," she said with a blush. "It's just, these kinds of conversations don't normally happen."

"They seem to with this family more often than not," Mitchell added dryly.

Brandon let out a breath and continued. "I think the moon goddess needed me to know this because, somehow, I'm connected to the wards." He looked at Kameron and Walker. "Every time the wards flare, and their power weakens, it hurts me. Is it the same with you?"

They were both still for a moment before nodding as one. Brandon let out a breath, relieved and terrified of what that meant.

Gideon growled. "And none of you thought to tell us?"

Walker cleared his throat. "I didn't know what it meant."

"I still don't," Kameron bit out. "I was handling it just fine."

Avery squeezed Brandon's hand. "So was Brandon, at least he thought he was. Maybe none of you told the others for a reason, but now it's out there."

"And I think I know why," Brandon interjected. "The moon goddess also told me of a prophecy."

Parker's gaze shot to his, his eyes wide. "Are you serious?"

Brandon nodded. "I didn't tell you right away because it didn't feel like the right time."

Parker growled. "Since I kept it secret, as well, I'll let you off this once."

Gideon snarled. "Why doesn't everyone tell me what the fuck is going on with my family?"

Brandon let out a breath. "I think the three of us,"—he pointed at himself, Walker, and Kameron—"are connected to the wards because we were the ones who helped build the first ones. At least, our past-life selves were." He winced. "That sounds weird now that I say it aloud."

Parker snorted. "We've passed weird so many times, it's pretty normal now. And Brandon? I don't think it was just the three of you who made the wards. It had to be my great-great-great—times a hundred—grandfather, too, right? I mean, if he was the first wolf, then the four of us, or maybe more, made the first wards."

"And that means we need to be the ones to fix them," Brandon added softly.

"I hear what you're saying, but what is this prophecy

you're talking about?" Finn asked, his hand linked with Brynn's.

Parker was the one who spoke.

"*A wolf of three Packs can break their will or unite them all.*

"*Once united, the Packs will reveal...*

"*If broken, the Packs will fall...*"

Brie's hand went to her mouth. "A wolf of three Packs...that's...that's Parker. Right?" Her eyes filled with tears, and she sniffed. "Hormones. Sorry. But, Parker. You're a Talon now, though your mother was a Talon before she left. You were raised a Redwood and..." She trailed off, and those who remembered the great war between the Redwoods and Centrals sucked in a breath.

"And I'm the son of the Central's Alpha. The one who killed countless people for power. So, yes, it would seem I'm the wolf of three Packs. But I don't know how I can help us." He shook his head before letting out a breath. "And that's not the first time I've heard the prophecy either."

After he'd told the others of what had happened in the European Pack—though some already knew part of it—the room quieted as they tried to digest everything that had just happened.

Avery cleared her throat and Brandon looked down at

her, worried. "There's something else, something I need to tell all of you. Something that Parker and Brandon know but I've been holding back. Not because I wanted to keep it a secret, but because...well...everything keeps happening so *fast*."

Hell, they'd all been so worried about everything else, they'd forgotten this one thing that could help.

"What is it?" Gideon asked, his voice low, his eyes narrowed.

He and Parker reached out and gripped her hands and she immediately let out a breath. "I'm a foreseer," she whispered. Parker squeezed her hand. "I can see a future," she continued, this time a little louder. He was so damned proud of her. "Not all futures and usually not those too close to me, but I have visions that can come true. I can't always figure out what each of them means, but I try to help those I can."

Gideon let out a breath. "That's a heavy burden, Avery."

His stomach eased, so freaking relieved that his brother and his Pack understood his mate as well as he did. "It is, but I carry it. And I'll do everything I can to help us. I promise."

Mitchell leaned forward, a frown on his face. "What do you see, Avery?"

She pressed her lips together before letting out a breath. "Blood. Screams. And Death."

Silence.

"What does it all mean?" Brie asked, her voice soft, breaking into the silence.

"I don't know," Brandon said honestly. "But something's coming. Something beyond human intervention and laws. The moon goddess is *mad,* and I think she's going to do all in her power to make sure no one messes with her wolves again."

Parker met Brandon's eyes, and they both blew out a breath. "And if that happens, I just pray our Packs aren't in the way."

Because if a goddess intervened, the world might truly end. But if she didn't...everything Brandon held dear might just end anyway.

CHAPTER 17

PARKER KISSED BRANDON SOFTLY before the other man said his goodbyes and went to visit Brie. Now that Brandon seemed somewhat whole, he wanted to ensure that he was fulfilling his Omega duties to the fullest. Parker, however, was still worried about the ward flares. At least other people knew about them now, and Brandon wouldn't be alone if something happened.

Still, the worries going through Parker's mind kept wrapping over and under one another, combining into this giant ball of anxiety that he wasn't sure he knew how to overcome.

Then Avery put her hand on his chest, and he could breathe again.

Goddess, he'd never known he could love someone as much and as deeply as he did her and Brandon. He might have gone through hell to get here, but he would *never* take his love for Avery and Brandon for granted. Their mating bond flared, and he knew Avery was thinking of him, too.

The world might be ending, but in this room, with this woman, he was one damned lucky wolf.

He looked down at her, her eyes wolf and her lips parted. "You're so beautiful."

She snorted, and he fell more in love with her. "You're crazy. I just finished training with you and Brandon, and I have sweat in places I don't want to think about. Plus, I don't think I've washed my hair in like four days since Ryder and Mitchell want me to read all the books about our history since I'm now a maternal dominant. I'm going a little stir crazy too because I can't leave the den, and I haven't even been here a fraction as long as most of you guys. So, yeah, I don't know what you're smoking to think I'm beautiful right now, but...thank you."

He kissed her hard to shut her up, loving the way she growled into his lips. When he pulled away, they were both panting. "You're beautiful no matter how much gunk you have in your hair."

He sent a wave of love through the mating bond even as she punched him in the arm for his words. She pulled back, her eyes wide.

"I *felt* that."

He lowered his head, taking her lips again. "Want to feel something else?"

She threw her head back and laughed. "That was such a cheesy line." She paused. "But I still want to do you, so the line must have worked." She kissed him hard, and he wrapped his arms around her. "I want to forget about the world for just a little while, can you do that?"

He palmed her ass, giving it a squeeze. "I can do that, mate of mine. I can do that."

She kissed him hard, and he somehow made it back to the bedroom, wanting more space so he could splay her out and have his way with her. He quickly stripped off her clothes, needing her naked flesh under his touch. When she reached between them to help him strip, he let her tug and pull, laughing with her when the fabric tore.

"Still not used to your strength?" he teased.

She bit his shoulder, and his wolf howled. "You mean you don't think I could have done that before when I was human?"

Parker kissed her again, molding her breasts with his hands. She arched into him, letting out a gasp of surprise when he pinched her nipples with more force than he usually gave her. Instead of pulling away, she pressed closer to him.

"I don't know what you did as a human, but I don't care at the moment since my dick is about to sink into your wet heat. You want it hard, Avery? You want me to fuck you hard right into the mattress so you're screaming my name as you come and milk my dick?"

She reached between them and stroked him. He thrust into her hold, wanting more. "Make it as hard as you want, Parker. Show me what you've got."

He grinned, and he knew from the way her eyes widened, he looked feral. "Good."

He picked her up and tossed her on the bed in a blink before moving so he straddled her upside down. Parker licked between her legs, and Avery started sucking his cock at the same time, causing both of them to moan and yet not lose their rhythm.

He hummed against her clit even as he used his fingers to spear her. He kept his hips steady, though, letting her control how she wanted to use her mouth since this position could end up hurting them both.

When her hips started to come off the bed, he pinned her down and growled against her clit, biting down right after.

"Parker!"

She came on his face, and he licked her up, needing to know once again what she tasted like when she climaxed. Before she could start sucking him again, however, he slid off her and padded around to the edge of the bed.

"Flip over, babe."

She gave him a lazy look and started to roll over onto her stomach.

"Taking too long. Need to be in you." He gripped her by the hips and made sure she was on her stomach before pulling her down to the edge of the bed.

"Holy fuck, impatient much?" She shot him a look over her shoulder, but laughter danced in her eyes.

"Your pussy is wet and empty, and my dick needs to get inside you. So, yeah, I'm kind of impatient. Now get that ass in the air, and keep your face on the mattress, baby. I told you I was going to fuck you hard."

She practically purred and shook her hips as she lifted her butt. He gripped those hips of hers with a punishing hold and slammed into her in the next instant.

"Holy shit," she breathed. "A little warning next time."

He smacked her ass. "You got your warning, wolf of mine. And you liked it. I can feel you clenching my cock right now."

"Shit," she repeated but pressed back into him so her curves were flush with his hips.

"Now, hold on, Avery."

"If you say it's gonna be a bumpy ride, I'm gonna choke," she teased.

"Can't choke without my cock in your mouth." They both laughed, and he fell that much more in love with her.

Sex was *supposed* to be fun. Yeah, it was also sexy and sweaty and full of countless other emotions he couldn't name, but without the pleasure that came with making someone you love smile, it just wasn't the same.

A grin still on their lips, he pulled out of her before slamming back home. She groaned along with him, her hands fisting on the bedspread. He pistoned into her, his body shaking as his moves became more aggressive, his wolf rising to the forefront. When he put one foot on the edge of the bed to get a deeper angle, Avery began to move with him, meeting him thrust for thrust.

"I need to see your face," he growled after she came yet again.

He pulled out of her and flipped her onto her back so her legs were draped over his shoulders, and his hands were still on her hips. When he entered her again, she arched her back, playing with her nipples.

"That's it, Avery. Play with yourself. Imagine they're my hands." He grinned wickedly. "Imagine they're Brandon's."

At that image, they both screamed, coming hard as one. He pulled out of her soon after and wrapped his arms around her as he fell back onto the bed, trying to catch his breath.

"We need to do that again," she teased. "Over and

over. Because I never knew laughing during sex could be such a turn-on."

He shook his head and kissed her lazily. "You're only to laugh at jokes, Avery girl. Just saying."

She rolled her eyes. "You make me happy, Parker. You and Brandon." They both sobered, and he played with her hair, needing to touch her in even the smallest of ways. "I know it's going to get scarier, and I feel like something's coming that's going to change everything, but you and Brandon make me so happy. I don't want to lose that."

He held her close as their bodies cooled and their wolves slumbered. "We won't," he promised, his mate drifting off in his arms. "We won't."

He just hoped he hadn't lied.

CHAPTER 18

"I'VE NEVER SEEN SO many Alphas in once place," Parker whispered in Brandon's ear. Brandon nodded, his eyes on the wolves in front of him as he took in what danger could be lurking right beneath the surface.

"I'm glad Avery isn't here with us," Brandon said just as quietly.

"I agree."

"I mean, I know she can take care of herself but..."

"But having so many dominant, male wolves around us when we're newly mated would only aggravate our wolves." Parker's words were true, but Brandon had a feeling if they were to say them to Avery, she'd punch them, hard. And probably not in the arms like usual.

They were at the older building they'd been renovating off and on over the past year. It sat in the neutral zone between the Talon and Redwood dens and had once been part of the Central den. The Centrals were no longer a Pack, so they didn't have any claim to the land.

Though Brandon had a feeling that might not be exactly the case after their meeting today.

The building had also been where the initial council meetings between the Talons and Redwoods took place before they'd moved them to alternate between the dens as their Packs became more and more unified. It was also where they met with the Covens to make sure the witches were on board with whatever the wolves planned.

Today, there were no witches or true council members present.

Today, it was a meeting between certain key wolves of three Packs and one former Pack.

The Redwoods and Talons were there as usual, but this time, the Aspens had decided to send their Alpha and a lieutenant rather than anyone else in the hierarchy to meet with them. That, apparently, hadn't surprised Parker too much as he knew the Aspens moderately well, and yet knew they held more secrets than most Packs would ever hope to. Brandon hadn't known what to say to that when his mate had mentioned it, so he'd let it pass. There were some things that the three of them would have to keep private until their mating bond settled into place. And even then, he wasn't sure that everything would be fully revealed.

Two more wolves were joining them today, and they had surprised the hell out of Parker. These two were former Central wolves, who had hidden most of the children of the Pack years ago under Parker's father's reign. Brandon didn't know exactly how these adults had done it all those years ago, but he knew that they were the ones who had saved Charlotte's life, in addition to countless others.

The Centrals weren't a Pack anymore, but Brandon had a feeling things might change. Things were shifting so fast these days that it was hard to keep up.

"Come on," Parker said softly, though every wolf around them could hear the words. There were no such things as whispers in a roomful of shifters with enhanced hearing. Brandon followed Parker and took a seat next to him.

Mitchell and Gideon sat on the other side of Brandon, his Alpha's tension at an all-time high. Brie had forced her mate to come to this because it was his duty as Alpha, even though he would have rather been by her side. She'd apparently gotten really growly and angry and had pushed him out of the house, even while kissing him on the mouth and making sure he knew he was loved and the baby would be okay. Brandon honestly had no idea how

Brie had accomplished that feat, but Gideon was here now, wolf prowling right under his skin. Brie was tucked in bed at home with Walker watching her every move. If she finally went into labor, everyone would stop the meeting. Even if they weren't getting along with the Aspens at the moment, their asshole Alpha understood the significance of pregnant mates.

"Let's get on with it," Kade said after a few moments of tense silence. It had been a long time since so many Alphas had met like this, and there were technically only three of them since the Centrals hadn't been goddess-blessed with an Alpha as of yet.

The only reason these wolves had even been allowed to be part of this meeting was because of what they'd done for their children during the last war. They had sacrificed their lives and everything they'd once held dear to protect the young ones under their care, and for that, Kade and Gideon had allowed the Centrals to attend. Blade, the Aspen Alpha, had not been invited into the decision, as he hadn't aided in the war.

Brandon wasn't sure how Blade felt about that. In fact, he wasn't sure what Blade felt at all. While his powers as an Omega didn't extend to wolves and humans outside his Pack, he could usually glean some emotions from them. Blade just bled asshole through and through.

"I still don't know why we're meeting in public like

this," Blade spat. "Unlike the two of you, my Pack isn't out in the open."

Brandon gripped Parker's thigh as his mate growled so low that only the two of them could hear. Parker was supposed to be the calm one of the group, and yet Brandon had a feeling Parker wasn't in the mood to deal with Blade. Hell, *Brandon* wasn't in the mood to deal with the Aspen Alpha. And dealing was kind of his thing.

"The government knows about your Pack, Blade," Gideon growled. "Don't try and deny that. They've known about all of us for years, but it's been in their best interests to keep it from the public."

"Until your old Pack members decided to fuck with all of us," Blade shot back.

Brandon clenched his jaw. His uncle had started the Unveiling, but Brandon's Pack hadn't been the only one over the past few years to be outed. It had just taken one domino to fall for more and more wolves and witches to be forced out into the open.

"If you're done acting like a petulant child, Blade, we can actually get things done," Mitchell put in, his voice low.

Brandon pinched the bridge of his nose. The only reason he was even there while most of the others had only brought one or two wolves with them was that he was here as Parker's mate. Technically, as Voice of the

Wolves, Parker was a mediator, but Brandon had never seen Parker work. He had a feeling they wouldn't get much accomplished today no matter what.

This was hopefully the first of many face-to-face meetings, but with the way Blade was acting, and the fact that the Central representatives hadn't said much, Brandon wasn't sure what the next step would be.

Gideon growled low, his wolf so close to the surface Brandon could practically see it prowling beneath his brother's skin. The room quieted, as if even the most dominant of predators knew they could become prey in Gideon's midst.

"I need to go to my mate, but instead, I'm sitting here listening to growling and rambling that won't accomplish anything." He took a deep breath, and Brandon did what he could to siphon off the rage and anxiety from his Alpha. It wasn't easy with Gideon usually since his brother kept himself locked-up with everyone except for Brie, but today, Gideon was about ready to explode.

Parker leaned forward, and Brandon squeezed his mate's knee, sending any support he could. "The wards are failing. You know this as much as I do. And no matter what the witches within our Packs do, they cannot stop the fall. Once the wards are no more, we will no longer be hidden from those who want to watch us. To harm us. Right now, every time the wards flash, every time the magic buckles, they get glimpses of our location, and our people become less and less safe."

He paused and looked to Brandon.

"And it's not just the wards," Brandon added. "Once this proposed agenda goes through Congress, we could lose our rights to live as we do."

"We've been here longer than this country has," Blade growled. "And maybe it's time they recognize that."

Brandon shook his head. "They *do* recognize that. And that's why some of them are scared."

"They want us for power," Parker said. "They want us because they either want what we have, or they don't want us to have it at all. Those who fear us don't understand us. And those who are on our side, who want us to live as we always have—just not under the veil of secrecy any longer—aren't loud enough in the grand scheme of things."

"And even though we've placed our people in high-level positions around the country, it's not enough when senators like McMaster are the loudest," Gideon added.

"Then what do you suppose we do?" Blade asked, anger in his eyes.

"We stand as one. We protect one another. We find a way to rebuild the wards." Brandon didn't tell the Aspen Alpha about the prophecy. Though he had spoken of unity, Brandon *knew* if he told Blade about the prophecy, it would put Parker in danger.

One of the Central wolves cleared his throat. "We aren't a Pack, not technically. We have meager wards that protect the youngest—a gift from the moon goddess herself. And I don't know what will happen to us in the future, but we stand with you." He looked directly at Parker as he said it, and Brandon once again squeezed his mate's knee.

Parker was the eldest son of their former Alpha and could have been Alpha of the Centrals if things had happened differently throughout history, but war changed everything.

"You killed our wolf, Gideon," Blade accused. "You killed Henry, and yet we're supposed to stand by your side? Instead of vengeance, I have to look at Henry's murderers and sit beside them at this table. He calls himself the Voice of the Wolves, but he's a murderer."

Brandon growled, going to his feet in the next instant. Gideon held up a hand, his body shaking with rage.

"Sit down," Gideon said low, and Brandon sat, his claws poking from his fingertips. "We've discussed this, Blade. Your wolf was rogue. You know this. You told me he had been missing for over a *year* when he came to our den. And we both know it wasn't a coincidence. Someone was holding him until that exact moment."

Blade stood up, his wolf in his eyes. "I'm not going to listen to these lies any longer. Our Pack is still hidden and will be as long as you Talons and Redwoods don't fuck it up again for the rest of us. Clean up your mess."

He stormed out, taking his other wolf with him, and Brandon closed his eyes.

"Jesus Christ that man is a fucking idiot," Kade growled once Blade was out of earshot. "We needed this meeting if only to see the man face-to-face, but hell, I don't know how you do this, Parker."

Brandon's mate snorted. "Usually, I'm on their turf, and they parade around like damned peacocks. Not all of the Alphas are as extreme as Blade, though. The man is slowly going off his rocker."

Brandon let out a breath. "I hope their Pack is strong enough then to deal with that." He met his brother's eyes, but Gideon had stiffened before Brandon could say anything.

All at once, Gideon stood, just as his phone rang. "Brie's in labor."

"Your phone didn't even ring—" Parker started before cursing. "Mating bond?"

Mitchell took the phone from Gideon's hands since the Alpha was about to go wolf. "You run quicker in wolf form than human, and you're a hell of a lot faster than our car when you get going. Go. I'll be right behind you. Let me text Walker that you're on your way."

Gideon was gone before Mitchell had even finished his sentence, Parker right behind him. Of the three Talons left in the room, Parker was the fastest and could probably keep up with Gideon.

Brandon turned to Kade, who had a broad smile on his face. "I'll let Jasper and Willow know their daughter is in labor, but knowing them, they already know. Those two and Brie's sisters will be the only ones heading over right now since I figure Gideon might not do too well with so many outside wolves in his territory at the moment."

Mitchell snorted. "Sounds about right. Though with so many matings between us, and new babies on the way, you never know."

The two Central wolves stood next to their table, looks of quiet contemplation on their faces. Everything that had been said so far had been common knowledge, but Brandon had a feeling these two were soaking everything in, feeling represented for the first time in over thirty years.

Brandon ran a hand through his hair, wondering how everything could change so quickly. One minute, they were trying to discuss a plan for the wards; the next, a new life was about to come into the world.

"We should go," Mitchell said quietly to Brandon before heading out without another word.

Brandon nodded at Kade and the others before following his cousin out the door. Kade would speak to the Centrals about what would happen next. Though the Redwoods had a tricky and complicated relationship with the wolves belonging to no Pack, Kade had never treated those who saved the innocent with anything but respect. Brandon wasn't sure what would happen next with them, but he had a feeling this meeting was only the beginning. And as for the Aspens? Brandon *knew* Blade wouldn't walk away as easily as he'd done today again.

As with the Centrals…this was only the beginning.

Brandon rolled his neck over his shoulders as he shifted on the uncomfortable chair. Why all waiting rooms in infirmaries had to have uncomfortable chairs was beyond him.

Avery sat to his left, nervously tangling her fingers when she wasn't holding his hand. Parker paced in front of him, worry for his cousin evident on his face. Brandon sometimes forgot that even though Brie, Charlotte, and Parker were Talons now, they were also cousins from the Redwood Pack. They'd known each other for most of their lives and were closer than some siblings were thanks to their ages.

"First births take a long time sometimes," Brynn said from Finn's lap. "But it shouldn't be too long, right?" Her mate kissed her temple and rubbed a hand over her stomach. Interesting.

She and Finn had shown up along with Brie's immediate family. Though Kade had said only the latter would be showing up, Brandon figured he'd forgotten that his son's mate was also the sister of the Talon Alpha. Their families were seriously confusing sometimes.

Every single person in this room was going to somehow be related to this baby, and Brandon couldn't help the smile tugging at his lips.

"What?" Avery asked. "Why are you smiling?"

"This kid is going to have so much family watching over him or her that they aren't going to know what to do with themselves."

Avery's smile widened. "Between the two Packs, they're going to have like forty close family members making sure they're safe. I like that."

Parker turned to them, a smile on his face, as well. "And don't forget, this child will one day be Alpha. So he or she is going to want to take care of everyone else, as well."

Brandon laughed. "I can't wait to see Gideon holding

a squalling baby Alpha." He froze, a tiny new bond wrapping around his heart. He sucked in a breath as he recognized who this new thread belonged to. When he turned to those in his Pack that held similar connections to his Omega ones, smiles broke out on their faces.

"You won't have to wait long," Walker said as he entered the room. "Gideon and Brie are holding their new child now, but soon, they'll bring our one-day Heir and Alpha out to be introduced."

"Don't keep us waiting," Jasper, Brie's father, said with a grin. "My mate is in there with them and won't tell me a thing."

Walker winked. "I think Gideon and Brie should be the ones to tell you." He looked at Mitchell, Brandon, Ryder, and Kameron and snorted. "Though some of you already know."

"Well, damn it," Max grumbled with a laugh. "These are the days I wish I had a special power like you guys."

"Tell me about it," Brynn said with a smirk.

Walker moved out of the way as Gideon strode inside, a tiny bundle wrapped in a pale, dove grey blanket in his arms.

"I wanted Brie out here with me," Gideon said softly, his gaze on his child. "But she and her mother are getting her comfortable and she didn't want me to wait to introduce you to your new Pack member."

He looked up, his wolf in his eyes, along with tears. "Everyone, meet Fallon, our daughter."

The room went silent for a bare moment before they rushed forward as one to greet their new one-day Heir and Alpha.

Fallon.

A daughter.

One day, a woman would rule the Talons, and Brandon thought it was about damned time.

LASTING

McMaster did not like to be kept waiting. He'd waited ten years after learning of the shifters' existence, only to have Montag act too rashly and almost derail his entire plan. He'd spent countless hours researching how Packs worked and how he could use the knowledge to his advantage.

Finally, *finally*, after all his long years of painful waiting, he was almost at the pinnacle of his plans. He would use the anger and fear of the people to catapult him into the presidency and the history books forever. That was what he wanted.

Power.

Legacy.

And the wolves would be the ones to give it to him.

But the people were faltering. They were taking far too long to get on board with his plan. They were starting to see the wolves as *people*. As humans who could have children and jobs and do everything normal people could do but who also happened to shift into an animal; a beast the public apparently thought the wolves could control.

The hate groups were backing away from attacking the dens straight on because the wolves fought back. And since they had claws and teeth, they could win. McMaster didn't understand how people were suddenly okay with these abominations.

The government, as always, was working at a snail's pace to put forth the legislation that would aid McMaster. And because of all of this, he was starting to lose ground in the polls.

The current President might just *beat* him after doing *nothing* to protect the people of this great nation from the hordes of wolves that could kill them with one blink.

McMaster let out a breath. His first splinter cell outside of Montag had been killed too easily. He hadn't sent enough men from his mercenary payroll, and now they were dead, and McMaster needed more ammunition. More momentum.

It seemed he might have to actually do something himself this time to ensure that his plan actually worked. He might be putting more into this last battle than he'd originally planned on, but soon, it wouldn't matter.

Soon, the Talons would be dead, and McMaster

would be there to pick up the pieces and show the world that he was the only one who could lead them through this horror.

    Soon, the world would see.

    Soon.

MITCHELL

Mitchell refused to show weakness to those who could still be his enemy, but today, he didn't have a choice. Even though he was a shifter and could heal faster than humans and survive injuries others could not, he was still limping after the shot that had hit his femoral artery.

Apparently, his injury had been worse than they'd thought, and he was lucky to be alive. And since Walker couldn't fully Heal him thanks to whatever had gone wrong with the wound, Mitchell would be limping for a bit longer yet. He just hoped it wasn't permanent. Because while he might still have the same strength he did before and could still fight in a battle, he couldn't let the other Packs know that the Talon Pack Beta had been injured.

He let out a breath, ignoring the ache in his leg that

echoed through the hollowness in his chest and made his way to the lone sentry at the Central's den. Though they weren't a full Pack yet as they hadn't been blessed by the moon goddess with an Alpha or any of the other hierarchy members, they had wards and children to protect, so it made sense that they would at least have a sentry.

From the look of him, however, Mitchell had a feeling this man needed much more training to be of any use.

Many of the Central members who had hidden their young all those years ago had left to find full Packs to join. Not many Packs would take them in unless they had young, and no one had come to the Talons for aid. Considering the Talon's former Alpha, Mitchell didn't blame them.

But Mitchell had a feeling if these wolves weren't blessed by the moon goddess soon, *all* of them would have to leave for other Packs. He wasn't sure why they hadn't yet, but there had to be a reason.

And that reason was the motivation for him being there now. That and to ensure they were ready for what might come soon. They were located close enough to the Talon den that if another battle broke out, they might get caught in the crossfire. Gideon didn't want these people to die because they weren't strong enough yet and couldn't fight for themselves. Only Mitchell didn't know what they were going to do next for their own Pack, let alone these other wolves with no home of their own.

The sentry gave him one look and let him slide through the weakening wards. He shook his head, holding back a curse. Hell, the Talon wards were getting closer and closer to failing, and yet they were still far stronger than these. He *knew* that if McMaster and the others were aware of the Centrals, these wolves would be slaughtered in a matter of moments.

His wolf growled, *needing* to protect those who couldn't protect themselves.

The man almost wondered why it would matter.

He hadn't been able to protect *her* in the end.

How could he protect anyone else?

DAWN

Dawn watched as the man strode into the Central's den, his chin held high. If it weren't for the minuscule limp she spotted, she'd have thought him an invincible force. The fact that he seemed hurt made her feel a little less on the defensive about his presence.

She was a wolf with no Pack, just a den with a name that had once caused the deaths of hundreds before she'd been born. And yet this man had come to them just now, and she didn't know why.

Was he there to kill them after all this time?

Or was he there to help them?

No one had helped them for so long, and Dawn knew it was her Packs' penance. They helped themselves, their weak and submissive wolves the majority as they didn't have many—if any—true dominants anymore.

She looked over at the man one last time, aware that he hadn't yet glimpsed her. She didn't know why he was here, but she knew, *knew*, that him being there was an omen.

Her wolf pushed at her as if scenting a danger she couldn't. She looked around at the same time the man did and froze.

The wards pulsated around them. Once. Twice.

Before they *fell*.

They were open to the world, to any eye that wanted to glimpse them. No amount of magic would save them.

The wards had fallen.

And from the look of horror on the man's face, it wasn't just her wards.

All the wards had fallen.

All of them.

CHAPTER 19

AVERY LET OUT a scream as the wards fell around them. Whatever bonds connected the Pack to the wards that usually protected them were ripped from within her, leaving her a tattered mess of agony.

Brandon went to his knees at her feet, and she followed him, holding him to her. Blood seeped from his nose as he coughed, trying to catch his breath, and she ran her hand down his back, at a loss for what to do. They'd been walking back from training and were only a few feet from their home, but she knew she wasn't strong enough yet to pick him up and carry him inside on her own.

Parker ran up to them, his brother Blake by his side, shouting. "The wards fell," he said with a growl. "And, of course, fate has decided it's the perfect time for another fucking splinter cell to attack us."

Blake cursed. He'd been visiting Brie that morning and had wanted to stay with Parker for a bit while the rest of the family had gone back home. "Dad texted to say the wards fell at the Redwoods, too."

"And Mitchell said the Centrals, as well," Parker put in as he knelt down beside the two of them. "I think Gideon is going to be hearing from more Alphas soon. This can't just be the three Packs near here."

Avery cupped Brandon's face, aware that the others were speaking around her about what their next step should be, but didn't really hear any of it, she needed to make sure her mate was okay.

"Brandon? Talk to me." She wiped the blood that had dribbled to his chin and blinked back tears.

"I'm okay," he said after a moment, clearing his throat. "It only hurt for that moment, but it was awful. Walker and Kameron are probably going through the same thing."

She looked over at Blake. "Did you feel anything when the wards fell?" she asked, wondering about something.

He nodded. "But it was just a soft whoosh. Not anything like what Parker felt." He winced. "Sorry if I wasn't supposed to say anything about that."

Avery pressed her lips together. The boy might be a man and about her age, but he still felt so much younger to her. She didn't want him in whatever fight was to come, but she had a feeling there might not be a choice.

"I think you two must have taken some of the pain from me," Brandon said as he stood on shaky legs. "Walker and Kameron don't have mates, so they took the full brunt of it."

"But you still feel them, right?" Parker asked, and Brandon nodded. "Then they're alive and will be on their feet soon. We need to be out there to protect the den."

Gideon ran to them at that moment, his wolf glowing in his eyes. "Brie and the submissives are hunkering down in the bunker." He turned to Avery. "The maternal dominants are either with them or are going out into the field with us. It's up to you which you want to do, but you're fighting stronger these days and you do better when you're with your mates." He looked at his family, and Avery lowered her gaze, his presence so *Alpha* at that moment that she could barely breathe. Others gathered around them, and she gripped her mates' hands. Blake stood behind her and put his hand on her shoulder as if he knew she needed to know *all* of her new family was there and okay. At least, for now.

Gideon looked around the crowd, and Avery let out a breath, not knowing how she'd come to be here, how she'd fallen for these people so quickly. Yet she *knew* this had been her fate. This day had been the one from her dreams, the event in her visions. She'd known this day would come where they would fight for their families and Packs, not knowing what would come after.

She'd seen the horror.

Now she had to live it.

"We know what to do," Gideon said. "We've trained. Our people are strong. We are more than our claws, more than our wolves, we are *everything*. Fight alongside your sisters and brothers and mates and show the world that we protect what is ours. If this is the end, then we fight for those who cannot fight for themselves. Our Pack is in danger, our den threatened, and those we love need us to show those who would kill us that we are tougher, far stronger than they imagine. Fight with me, Talons. Fight for your Pack. Fight for your people. Fight for yourselves."

Avery threw her head back at her Alpha's words and howled, not knowing *how* she knew to do that with the others, but going on instinct. She wasn't a human any longer, she was one of the Pack.

And she would fight.

As the others mobilized, their training showing, Parker cupped her face and kissed her, hard. Avery leaned into him, taking everything she could from the kiss. She loved this man, loved the other man by their side. She didn't want to die for them, but if fate called, she would do so.

Brandon pulled her away from Parker to kiss her before kissing Parker, as well—the three of them standing in a circle as she tried to come to terms with what was happening. Less than a minute had passed, and yet everything had changed.

"Fate brought me to you," she said suddenly. "And damn fate if she thinks she's going to take you away from me."

Parker kissed her hard again before moving back to grip Blake's shoulder. "Then let's make sure our people are safe. Fate isn't taking any of you away from me anytime soon."

Brandon nodded, his eyes wolf.

"Damn straight," Blake added as Tatiana ran to their group. She'd come to speak with Gideon about something. Whatever it was wasn't Avery's business and, frankly, Avery was happy to see Tatiana in fighting leathers with a gun strapped to her thigh.

"I don't have a team to fight alongside," Tatiana said, her wolf in her eyes. It seemed this woman had a far stronger wolf than Avery had thought. "May I fight alongside you?"

"Of course." It was Avery who answered. "Let's do this."

Max joined them, and the six of them gathered their weapons as they ran to where the majority of the fighting had started. Though Avery wasn't as good as the others, her mates were, and she could be the one reloading for them if she found herself in the way. But she was a damn good shot now, and she'd protect what was hers no matter what.

When they made it to the clearing, Avery's mouth dropped.

"There's so many," Tatiana whispered. "So many who hate our kind." Blake squeezed her shoulder, and Avery gripped the other woman's arm, feeling a solidarity that only came when one was facing death head-on.

"There are others who do not," Brandon said softly. "But they are not here to fight by our side, so we will do what we do best and be *wolves*."

Some had already shifted around them; their fighting techniques better in wolf form than human. Others were strapped with knives and guns—the idea they only needed to fight with tooth and claw long since passed in this new age of war.

Avery took in what was happening and knew not everyone would make it out alive. She *knew*. But she couldn't say anything, not when that would only make it inevitable. Her visions might be of the future, but that didn't mean they were the only future out there.

Her family could surprise her, but she needed to fight

for them. So she took the safety off her gun and let out a slow breath.

"We fight."

"We fight."

"We fight."

Another scream echoed off in the distance as one of the fully black-garbed unit members went down under Max's hold. Avery fought by the man's side, taking out the splinter cell members from far away since she was a better distance fighter than closer to the carnage.

Blake, Brandon, and Parker were only twenty feet away, going hand-to-hand with more than twice their numbers, winning, but bloodily. So many wolves fought near her against even more humans. She couldn't quite believe that it had come to this.

She'd known it had to, but it still didn't feel real.

Around them, the witches of their den used their magic to push the humans back, and the humans of their Pack either fought alongside them or were back with the children, keeping them safe. No member stood by and watched. Every single person with the Pack bonds permeating their body fought in some fashion to end the battle.

"That fucker McMaster is here," Max said with a grunt. He punched the guy coming at Avery in the face and growled. "Always knew he was shady, but it seems he's officially taken Montag's place." Max whirled around and faced Avery. "Shit. I forgot."

Avery shot the man coming at Max's back. "Forget it. My father was a sadistic bastard that killed anyone in his way. I'm glad he's dead." She shot another person coming at her before having to reload. "And McMaster isn't any better. He's staying out of sight of the cameras that are inevitably watching, but he won't be hidden for long."

Tatiana yelled as she took out another mercenary and came to Avery's side for more ammo. "He is a fekking loser who only uses his power for evil. The world will see him for who he is."

Avery laughed at the woman's surprising words then screamed as Tatiana's eyes widened. A circle of blood appeared on the other woman's chest, and blood sprayed over Avery's face as Tatiana fell to her knees.

"Fuck!" Max fell beside her and tried to stop the bleeding, but it was no use. A wolf could survive many things but a bullet wound directly to the heart was fatal no matter the strength of the person.

Tatiana was dead. The woman who had left the safety of her den to fight for others had died at the hands of a coward with a long-range rifle.

"Sniper!" Avery choked out. "Get down!"

There hadn't been a sniper yet as it had been hard for

the humans to find a position, but, apparently, they'd finally found one. Now, no one would be safe. There might not be a tank like last time, but her people were falling faster and faster.

Blink.

The wolf from the infirmary with a nice smile. Gone.

Blink.

The sentry she had first talked to when she'd come to the den. Gone.

Blink.

The maternal dominant male who had helped her learn how to use her wolf for the goodness of others. Gone.

Avery's tears salted her tongue as she dropped her now empty gun and launched herself at the nearest human who had decided her new family needed to die because of the blood that ran in their veins.

She stabbed at him with her knife, and though she now had faster reflexes, she was still too slow. The man grabbed her arm and twisted. When she called out, both Brandon and Max ran to her, claws out.

She was too new to use her claws but damn it, she didn't want to die this way. So she kicked out, hitting the asshole right in the balls. He let out a squeak before letting go. When he doubled over, she kicked him in the head.

"Holy hell, Avery," Max said with a pained grimace. "Remind me to never get on your bad side."

She opened her mouth to say something equally as inappropriate, but then the world went bright white before going black.

She pried open her eyes and screamed out in horror. The bomb that had gone off had sent so many of her family in different directions, she didn't know where to look. Brandon lay off to her side, struggling to get up.

Parker and Blake were too far away to have been hit by the blast, but they were running toward the melee.

But what made her scream was not her mates, but the one wolf who could always make her smile.

Max lay on his back, blood pooling around him on the grass, turning the green to rust. McMaster stood above him, a knife in his hand as he slashed at the unconscious wolf, a gleeful smile on his face.

"You're an abomination!" McMaster yelled. "Your kind is the reason our people are dying!" He slashed again.

Bile filled Avery's throat as she moved through the pain and saw Max's prone body in full. He no longer had any of his right arm below his elbow, as the blast must have taken it. But the wounds on his chest were worse as McMaster slashed and cut.

Why wasn't anyone shooting at him? Why couldn't anyone help? Her ears rang, and she knew others were coming toward them, but it wouldn't be quick enough. There wouldn't be enough time.

So she did the only thing she could.

She somehow found the strength to stand before leaping on McMaster's back. The man screamed and, thankfully, fell to the side and not on top of Max. The man who had been the root of so many of their problems rolled over and tried to get up, but his eyes widened as both of them realized what he'd fallen on.

The knife he'd used to hurt Max now lay embedded in his chest, his own life's blood pooling around the two of them.

"They'll know what you've done," McMaster spat, blood flowing from his mouth. "I'll still win."

"You'll be dead." She punched him in the face before staggering to Max, knowing there wasn't a lot of time. She cupped his face before reaching down and praying she'd find a pulse. When she felt the beat of his heart, she let out a sob and took off her jacket to staunch as much of the blood as possible.

"Walker!" she yelled. "We need you!" She had no

idea if the Healer was even still alive. She only knew that Max wouldn't survive without him.

Brandon fell to her side, blood and cuts covering his body and he pressed his hands down over hers. "Walker's coming, Avery. Walker's coming."

Parker ran past her, Blake right behind him as they made sure McMaster was dead. "He's dead. Killed by his own knife."

The man who had orchestrated it all was dead, yet Max still bleeding beneath her hands. Bullets still firing over her head. Why wasn't it over?

"I don't know what to do," Avery whispered. "I don't know what to do."

Parker leaned forward. "Walker's almost here," he whispered.

"Parker!" Blake yelled. "Get down!"

Then Avery was pushed onto Max as Parker slammed into her, Blake on top of both of them.

Avery knew that no matter how long she lived—if she survived this battle—she would never forget Parker's scream.

Never.

CHAPTER 20

PARKER LIFTED Blake's body off his and tried to come to grips with what he was seeing. His baby brother lay in his arms, his eyes wide with the surprise of death and blood covering his chest. Blake had taken a bullet meant for him, yet Parker didn't understand why.

Why.

Avery and Brandon would still have each other if Parker had died. Blake hadn't yet found his mate or mates. Damn it. His brother should still be there. He was supposed to fight by his side and make stupid jokes and help Parker clean up the mess. He'd wanted to watch Blake grow up into the man he was destined to become and eventually find his mate. Parker had thought he'd have Blake by his side when Isabelle found her mate so the two of them could be the typical big brothers and kick the man's ass if he did anything wrong or got too close.

He'd thought he'd have countless days with his little brother.

Blake should not be bleeding by his side, his eyes vacant as death took his due without recourse.

This was not his fate.

The moon goddess had lied.

She'd taken everything.

And Parker didn't know what to do.

Walker came forward at that instant and pushed the others out of the way to help Max. Avery ran her hands over Parker's face and down to Blake, tears streaming down her cheeks. Brandon stood behind him, shooting anything that came too close that didn't smell of Pack.

Yet Parker needed to get his head out of his ass and onto his family. His brother would *not* die in vain. Max would not lay bleeding in vain.

The prophecy whispered through his mind again, and he knew it was the moon goddess who spoke. The moon goddess who couldn't save his baby brother.

"*A wolf of three Packs can break their will or unite them all.*

"*Once united, the Packs will reveal...*

"*If broken, the Packs will fall...*"

"The wards," he gritted out, his hands covered in his and Blake's blood. "The wards."

Avery looked at him with confusion in her gaze as she tried to wipe the blood from his face. It didn't do much good since she had just as much blood on her hands. "What are you talking about?"

"My ancestor made the first wards. The witches were the ones to strengthen it. Maybe...maybe the goddess is saying it's me who will remake the wards." As soon as he said the words, he knew what he'd said was true.

Only, how?

He looked down at the blood on his hands that mixed with his brother's and knew the answer. "Blake and I are of the first hunter. It's our blood. His sacrifice." He choked out the words before slamming his hand to the ground. His brother's blood already seeped into the soil, and Parker used his free hand to claw at his own arm, making more blood pool into the grass and dirt.

"My blood," Parker growled out to the moon goddess. "Our sacrifice. *His* sacrifice. Take it and help us, damn it!" He knew it wasn't the right thing to say, wasn't as ritualistic as what the moon goddess might have liked, but his brother had died in his arms, and he couldn't think of anything else to say.

Avery looked at him with wide eyes before placing her hands on his. "Our blood. The blood of your mate."

Brandon did the same. "All of us. All of our life force. Take it. Protect our people."

"Unite us," Parker continued. "Save our Packs."

Thank you.

The moon goddess's words brushed over him as the wards slammed into place. Far more powerful than he'd ever felt them, they were like a bubble over the den area, thrusting deep into the earth and extending out to the surrounding roads and trees, creating the haven that had once been safe for all wolves. Parker let out a scream as power surged through him and into the wards, as if the moon goddess hadn't been able to do anything without this one moment.

He *felt* her power and grace create the wards, forming bonds within bonds as the den was once again not only hidden from view but also safe from those who would attack it.

Then the unbelievable happened.

The wards shot out, a wall of blazing hot magic going in all directions. Avery leaned into him and Brandon as the wards' power rushed forward, yet the immense heat didn't hurt them. Instead, it pushed every single one of their enemies away, a wall of fire and ice, protecting those it hadn't been able to fully protect for too long.

In the end, the Talons stood on the battlefield, their

bodies shaking from the new power sliding over their bodies. It was as if the wards had rejuvenated them. Max gasped below them as he opened his eyes, pain-bright, but Walker forced the wolf to go back to sleep to Heal.

Avery held Parker close, Blake's body still in his arms, and Brandon stood behind them still, protecting them from an enemy that seemed to have been knocked back by the moon goddess herself.

"You did it," Avery said, her voice raw.

"*We* did it," Brandon countered.

"But at what cost?" Parker asked, his throat aching. He held Blake to him as his mates comforted him. If he hadn't had Avery and Brandon by his side, he wasn't sure what he would have done.

The others moved around them, trying to understand what had happened as they took care of their wounded and dead.

But Parker stayed where he was, knowing it wouldn't be long before who he waited for appeared.

Because they would come. They would see.

The Redwoods arrived not long after, bringing Parker and Blake's parents with them. Lexi, Parker's mother, screamed, her body shaking as she ran toward them. North blinked at them, falling to his knees as he fully caught sight of the scene. It was his twin brother, Maddox, who lifted him up and helped him to where Avery, Brandon, and Parker kneeled, and Blake lay.

His family had come for their sons.

The battle had been won. The war, Parker knew, might end soon. The mastermind behind it all lay dead, and the world had seen what he'd done. The wards were back in place, stronger than ever.

But his brother was dead.

Countless had died.

Parker looked around at the bloodstained battleground, remembering the first battle he'd seen and the fire that had consumed so many. They had won that war, and Parker knew they would win this one. There was no other choice.

But no matter what he did in the future, he would not forget this day. His mates would not forget this day. The sacrifices that had been made on the battlefield would be forever remembered and honored.

His mates helped him stand as the others took Blake's body, and Parker wrapped himself around Avery and Brandon. Avery kissed his jaw, while Brandon kissed his temple.

Parker might have lost a part of himself in the battle, but in the arms of his mates, he found something else. He found his reason to fight, his reason to live. Blake wouldn't have wanted him to break down and hide. He hadn't sacrificed himself for Parker to do so. And for that, Parker would live.

But he would remember.

Always.

EPILOGUE

Two Days Later

BRANDON LAY in bed with Avery tucked to his side, Parker on the other side of her, his face finally calm in sleep. They'd made love for the first time since the battle that morning and now were taking a nap before they went to Gideon's home for a council meeting. They'd needed each other and to remember what they had fought for.

Avery let out a groan, and Brandon loosened his hold on her. Parker's eyes opened, and Brandon reached out to caress the man's hip softly.

They'd lost so much on the battlefield and yet had gained their new wards. Wards that seemed to be far stronger than anything anyone had seen in their long lives. It seemed that going forward in this new age of knowing and technology, their wards would be there to protect them from too curious eyes.

Blake had died protecting Brandon's mate, and he still didn't know how to deal with that. All he knew was that thanks to the man's sacrifice, they all had a long time to find a way to live with that. Tatiana had also died, though her Alpha had thankfully not blamed the Talons. Instead, the European Alpha had used her death as a way to come out to the public in his own territory. Her death, too, would not be in vain.

Max is alive, Brandon thought with a relieved breath. But he would never be the same physically, and from what Brandon had felt from his cousin in these short two days since the battle, he might never been the same emotionally either.

All in all, they'd lost twenty-seven wolves. But without the wards, the number of casualties would have been far greater.

Brandon closed his eyes, holding Avery and Parker closer as he fought to calm his wolf. He needed his mates by his side more now than he ever thought possible. He needed to constantly reassure himself that they were indeed alive and well and that he wasn't dreaming anymore.

Avery turned in his arms and kissed his chest before pressing her naked breasts to his skin. "You're thinking so loudly," she said softly. "Want to talk about it?"

Brandon swallowed hard as Parker ran his hand over Brandon's side. "I was just thinking about everything that happened." He paused. "And the fact that I think I'm still connected to the wards the same way I was before."

Parker sat up, a frown on his face. "It's not hurting you, is it?"

Brandon shook his head as he sat up, as well. Avery followed, tucking the sheet over her breasts. "No, but I can *feel* them."

Avery nodded. "I can, too." She bit her lip. "And I... uh, talked to Walker about it, and he said he still feels them."

"So does Kameron," Brandon added, running a hand down her back. "But I don't think it's quite the same with the others."

"So the three of you since you were already connected to the old ones through your past lives, and now those of us who helped Parker bring them back up?" Avery asked. "I guess that makes sense. I wonder what it means in the grand scheme of things?"

"I think it means we'll know when the wards need us again," Parker said slowly. He gave a rough laugh that had Brandon's eyes widening along with Avery's. "I can feel

Blake when I try to reach for the wards. It's like he'll always be here, you know?" He rubbed a fist over his chest. "I'm not going to get over what happened anytime soon, but I think...I think being in this Pack and being mated to the two of you is going to help me."

Avery kissed him on the cheek before turning to do the same to Brandon. "I think so, too." She let out a breath. "And I think we're going to be late to Gideon's if we don't get out of bed."

Brandon kissed the back of her neck. "I think he can wait just a bit longer." Parker leaned forward and kissed her on the lips, and the three of them laid back down, taking their morning slowly.

Because no matter what happened, Brandon would *never* take his mates and his fate for granted. It had cost so much to have the bond they shared, and he would do anything to keep it.

"WHAT HAPPENED ON THAT BATTLEFIELD IS A travesty. The shame of the man who ran for President will be a mark on our history for generations but will not define our history. He tried to use the fear of the unknown for his own gain, and in the end, it was to his peril."

Brandon sat wide-eyed on the couch between his mates as the President spoke to the public about what had happened to the Talons and what the future would hold when it came to the wolves.

"The proposed legislation against those who shift into wolves is unconstitutional, and I have been remiss in not making my statements clear. The shifters among us have been living within our borders for longer than our borders have been drawn. They have done nothing wrong, but they have been forced to hide for fear of what might happen to their children. And, as is evidenced by some of the corrupt people in power, their fears were justified. But know this, we are working to ensure that *all* people in our country and around the world are safe. That includes shifters."

"Holy shit," Avery whispered.

"Yeah," Parker added.

Brandon squeezed both of their hands.

"My daughter is the mate of a wolf from a Pack on the eastern seaboard," the President continued.

"Holy shit indeed," Gideon growled.

"And that's not one of the people we thought were on our side?" Mitchell asked. "The people we placed in command?"

"Nope," Gideon said. "We had no clue."

"You have followed my daughter's life since I came into politics and will continue to do so because you feel her life is fair game. I've always done my best to keep my family safe, and now her family includes the wolves of this country." He paused. "But before I knew of her future, I already knew what I would say now. Our people need to be safe. *All* of our people. The laws say so, as shifters within our borders *are* citizens. It is a crime to attack them for who they are. It has always been a crime, but those in power have not always seen that. *I* see that. We need to unite. We are a country built on coming together, and now we *will* come together. The wolves are under our protection. They are people. And they need to be allowed to take control of their own lives. Let's make sure we allow that to happen."

The President began to answer questions about what everything meant law-wise, but Brandon tuned it out, knowing they'd go over it in detail for years to come. Right then, he needed to focus on the two wolves in his arms.

"Does that mean we're safe?" Avery asked.

Gideon was the one who answered. "That means there will be no more human against wolf battles on our land." He looked down at his tablet as he read a few things from other Alphas and wolves around the country. "If a human faction comes at us, it will be our government that stands beside us to protect us."

"So, is the war over?" Brie asked, Fallon sleeping peacefully in her arms.

"This one, at least," Parker answered honestly, and the

others stared at him. "We're wolves. There's always going to be an aggressive stance somewhere, but we're not going to have to worry about what we've been dealing with for the past few years, at least."

Avery let out a sigh. "And the prophecy? I mean...did we save the world?"

Brandon snorted at her question. She narrowed her eyes at him, a small smile playing on her lips. "I think we've done what the prophecy wanted us to do, but who knows. It's a foretelling. Things tend to get confusing. But we weren't forced into silence. We found our voice. That counts for far more than just something."

The others started talking about the hundreds of things that were still on their plate just because the country had decided to protect them again, but Brandon kept his gaze on his mates. Avery leaned into him, and Parker kissed his temple.

"As curious as I am about what's going to happen, I think I'd rather hide with the two of you back at our place for a bit longer," Avery whispered.

Our place.

Goddess he loved that phrase. Out of the darkness, his happiness had crept up on him. He had not just one mate, but two, and a healthy Pack that would soon see countless sunrises and sunsets as they walked into a new world. The Talon Pack wasn't going anywhere anytime soon, and

Brandon knew he'd be right by his mates' sides in the coming days and years.

Their bonds were stronger than ever, and no matter what emotions rocked into him thanks to his mantle as Omega, or what places Parker needed to go because he was the Voice of the Wolves, or what obstacles Avery needed to face due to her new nature, they would do it together.

"I think going to our place sounds perfect," Brandon whispered.

"Perfect," Parker added.

Perfect was the right word. Their world might be far from it, but for now, he could use a little bit of perfect, and he could find that in the man and woman he loved.

THE END

Next in the Talon Pack World:
Mitchell and Dawn being a new era in Destiny Disgraced.

A NOTE FROM CARRIE ANN

Thank you so much for reading Fractured Silence! I do hope if you liked this story, that you would please leave a review! Reviews help authors and readers.

If you want to make sure you know what's coming next from me, you can sign up for my newsletter at www.CarrieAnnRyan.com; follow me on twitter at @CarrieAnnRyan, or like my Facebook page. I also have a Facebook Fan Club where we have trivia, chats, and other goodies. You guys are the reason I get to do what I do and I thank you.

Make sure you're signed up for my MAILING LIST so you can know when the next releases are available as well as find giveaways and FREE READS.

Happy Reading!

The Talon Pack:
- Book 1: Tattered Loyalties
- Book 2: An Alpha's Choice
- Book 3: Mated in Mist
- Book 4: Wolf Betrayed
- Book 5: Fractured Silence
- Book 6: Destiny Disgraced
- Book 7: Eternal Mourning
- Book 8: Strength Enduring
- Book 9: Forever Broken

ABOUT THE AUTHOR

Carrie Ann Ryan is the New York Times and USA Today bestselling author of contemporary, paranormal, and young adult romance. Her works include the Montgomery Ink, Redwood Pack, Fractured Connections, and Elements of Five series, which have sold over 3.0 million books worldwide. She started writing while in graduate school for her advanced degree in chemistry and hasn't stopped since. Carrie Ann has written over seventy-five novels and novellas with more in the works. When she's not losing herself in her emotional and action-packed worlds, she's reading as much as she can while wrangling her clowder of cats who have more followers than she does.

www.CarrieAnnRyan.com

ALSO FROM THIS AUTHOR

The Montgomery Ink: Boulder Series:
Book 1: Wrapped in Ink
Book 2: Sated in Ink
Book 3: Embraced in Ink
Book 4: Seduced in Ink
Book 4.5: Captured in Ink

The Montgomery Ink: Fort Collins Series:
Book 1: Inked Persuasion

The Less Than Series:
Book 1: Breathless With Her
Book 2: Reckless With You
Book 3: Shameless With Him

ALSO FROM THIS AUTHOR

The Elements of Five Series:
Book 1: From Breath and Ruin
Book 2: From Flame and Ash
Book 3: From Spirit and Binding
Book 4: From Shadow and Silence

The Promise Me Series:
Book 1: Forever Only Once
Book 2: From That Moment
Book 3: Far From Destined
Book 4: From Our First

The Fractured Connections Series:
Book 1: Breaking Without You
Book 2: Shouldn't Have You
Book 3: Falling With You
Book 4: Taken With You

Montgomery Ink: Colorado Springs
Book 1: Fallen Ink
Book 2: Restless Ink
Book 2.5: Ashes to Ink
Book 3: Jagged Ink
Book 3.5: Ink by Numbers

Montgomery Ink:

ALSO FROM THIS AUTHOR

Book 0.5: Ink Inspired
Book 0.6: Ink Reunited
Book 1: Delicate Ink
Book 1.5: Forever Ink
Book 2: Tempting Boundaries
Book 3: Harder than Words
Book 4: Written in Ink
Book 4.5: Hidden Ink
Book 5: Ink Enduring
Book 6: Ink Exposed
Book 6.5: Adoring Ink
Book 6.6: Love, Honor, & Ink
Book 7: Inked Expressions
Book 7.3: Dropout
Book 7.5: Executive Ink
Book 8: Inked Memories
Book 8.5: Inked Nights
Book 8.7: Second Chance Ink

The Gallagher Brothers Series:

Book 1: Love Restored
Book 2: Passion Restored
Book 3: Hope Restored

The Whiskey and Lies Series:

Book 1: Whiskey Secrets

ALSO FROM THIS AUTHOR

Book 2: Whiskey Reveals
Book 3: Whiskey Undone

The Talon Pack:
Book 1: Tattered Loyalties
Book 2: An Alpha's Choice
Book 3: Mated in Mist
Book 4: Wolf Betrayed
Book 5: Fractured Silence
Book 6: Destiny Disgraced
Book 7: Eternal Mourning
Book 8: Strength Enduring
Book 9: Forever Broken

Redwood Pack Series:
Book 1: An Alpha's Path
Book 2: A Taste for a Mate
Book 3: Trinity Bound
Book 3.5: A Night Away
Book 4: Enforcer's Redemption
Book 4.5: Blurred Expectations
Book 4.7: Forgiveness
Book 5: Shattered Emotions
Book 6: Hidden Destiny
Book 6.5: A Beta's Haven
Book 7: Fighting Fate

ALSO FROM THIS AUTHOR

Book 7.5: Loving the Omega
Book 7.7: The Hunted Heart
Book 8: Wicked Wolf

The Branded Pack Series:
(Written with Alexandra Ivy)
Book 1: Stolen and Forgiven
Book 2: Abandoned and Unseen
Book 3: Buried and Shadowed

Dante's Circle Series:
Book 1: Dust of My Wings
Book 2: Her Warriors' Three Wishes
Book 3: An Unlucky Moon
Book 3.5: His Choice
Book 4: Tangled Innocence
Book 5: Fierce Enchantment
Book 6: An Immortal's Song
Book 7: Prowled Darkness
Book 8: Dante's Circle Reborn

Holiday, Montana Series:
Book 1: Charmed Spirits
Book 2: Santa's Executive
Book 3: Finding Abigail
Book 4: Her Lucky Love

ALSO FROM THIS AUTHOR

Book 5: Dreams of Ivory

The Happy Ever After Series:
Flame and Ink
Ink Ever After

Single Title:
Finally Found You

Printed in Great Britain
by Amazon